P9-DCY-908

NAOMIS TOO

NAOMIS TOO

by Olugbemisola Rhuday-Perkovich & Audrey Vernick

BALZER + BRAY

An Imprint of HarperCollins*Publishers*

Balzer + Bray is an imprint of HarperCollins Publishers.

Naomis Too

ISBN 978-0-06-268515-5

Typography by Michelle Taormina
18 19 20 21 22   CG/LSCH   10 9 8 7 6 5 4 3 2 1
❖

First Edition

To the Brooklyn New School and Brooklyn School of Collaborative Studies communities. You never cease to inspire.

CHAPTER ONE

Naomi Marie

"Should I wear the jeans with the patchwork pockets?" I ask. "Or the purple skirt that I made? The zipper is kind of messed up, but I can cover that with my shirt." *First-day-of-school* outfits are so important. And first day of middle school is seriously momentous. It's the end of crayons and snack time, and the beginning of . . . a new era. I bet I'll get a smartphone for looking up word definitions! School dances like the ones on *Tidwell Academy* (at least that's what I've heard; I wouldn't know, since I'm not allowed to watch it)! A Teen section in the library! Not being with the same teacher all day! No Jenn Harlow! Woot!

Naomi E. takes a large bite of very jammy toast and looks at the outfits that I've laid out on my bed in our room. "I like the jeans," she says. "They look like you made an effort, but like you're the kind of person who makes an effort every day, not like you're trying too hard."

Years ago, I thought middle school was also going to mean My Own Room, because that's what my parents promised. And then it changed to My Own Room But Not at Dad's, because his apartment is Really Small. I love my little sister, but it was really good to dream about the day when I wouldn't have to hear Bri sing "You'll Sing a Song, and I'll Sing a Song" in ten languages until she fell asleep. Instead, now I have to step over a lot of . . . things on my way to my bed every evening. It's like an obstacle course. My new sister is just as messy in *our* new house as she was in *her* old one. Sigh.

"I forgot," I say, moving my clothes out of jam-dropping range. "I embroidered the pockets on the jeans, so it's semi-handmade. I was thinking of handmade clothes being my thing this year. What's yours going to be?"

"Sleeping in on Saturday mornings," Naomi E. says. "And doughnut hunting."

"Ha-ha," I say, handing her a tissue. "Hello? *Food-in-the-bedroom* rules? Seriously. Don't you think it's important to know in advance so that you can let people know who you are right away?"

She smiles and rolls her eyes at the same time, which is

something I've learned Naomi E. can do really well. "I think anyone can figure out who I am by, oh, I don't know, getting to know me if they want to."

"But people never want to! They judge and decide without giving you a chance to just . . . be."

"I think *you* don't give yourself a chance to just be."

It's one of those moments when there's so much to say that I don't say anything. Like how the principal made me take the Gifted test again because she didn't believe I could have "come by that score honestly." Or how in fourth grade Michael Tillerson asked me why I had a "normal" name like Naomi instead of a "Black" one.

I throw an emoji pillow in Naomi E.'s direction to change the topic. We finally convinced our parents to get them, but it took so long that they're not even cool anymore. But Naomi E. and I still like them. We have them all except the poop one, because why does that even exist.

"Seriously," says Naomi E., picking up the pillow and putting it on her bed. "You've got to relax. What could possibly go wrong?" She looks at the pillow. "Oops, I got jam on my laughy face."

Then we both laugh. Because, *duh*. We're the Naomis. Nothing's ever easy.

"Question," says Brianna, who has developed this habit of announcing her questions before she asks them. Makeda the

Marvelous, the main character from her favorite series, does it in every book.

In books, it's cute.

She turns to Naomi E., who is making herself a really thick turkey-and-cheese sandwich for lunch. "When school starts, should I call you White Naomi or Naomi E.?"

"Uh, Naomi E.'s fine, Bri. I think people will figure out that I'm white," answers Naomi E., and I laugh out loud. We went to a bunch of "multiracial family workshops" this summer, and it was a lot of stuff I already knew from Momma, but some new stuff too. We spent two whole sessions on whiteness, which I think we all know a lot about, but okay.

That's what our new "Yes, AND . . ." life is like. "Yes, this is my little sister, Brianna, AND my new sister, Naomi E." "Yes, the same name, AND we're the same age." "Yes, Tom is Momma's new husband, AND my dad lives a couple of subway stops away." Phew.

We've all been adjusting to life as *more* instead of *either/or.* More stuff in the closets, and more shelves because there weren't enough closets for the more stuff. No more time for books-and-bubble baths because more people have to use the bathroom. More votes for breakfast-for-dinner days, which are always fun. More working on making Naomi E. feel included. But sometimes it feels like that means I have to *exclude* myself.

The best of Yes, AND is when more means "Sure, girls,

we can go to Shelly Ann's AND Morningstar. Two bakeries in one day is awesome!"

We don't get that one so much.

"Anyway, silly, you won't see us during the school day," I say to Bri. "Kindergarten's on the first floor. We're in middle school now. Sixth graders are upstairs." Me and Naomi E. high-five.

"But you'll come visit me, right?" says Bri, and she looks a little scared even though she spent the whole summer bragging about being a "kid-nergardner," so I give her shoulders a quick squeeze. "Yeah, whenever I can, and if anybody bothers you, just tell them that your sister Naomi Marie is in sixth grade and she's got your back." We stand together back-to-back like we do every first day.

Naomi E. drops an apple into her lunch bag. "And me," she says. When we look at her, she adds, "I've got your back too."

It's still hard not to think of "me and Bri." We've always been a team of two. I'm used to being *the* big sister. I'm not sure how to be just *a* big sister. When we went to Coney Island over the summer, Naomi E. took Bri on a walk while I was on line to get clam strips. It was good not to have Bri squirming next to me saying "I'm hungry! I'm thirsty! I have to go to the bathrooooom!" the whole time, but I got a lump in my throat when I watched them walk away together, holding hands. And I don't think Naomi E. can help with some things, like flat twists. Does she even know what they are?

Momma rushes into the kitchen. "Ladies, we've got to go. We have two weeks for you to get this subway route down before you'll be going to school on your own."

"Maybe we could move that timeline up a smidge?" asks Naomi E. in a very sweet voice. "We've been talking and, uh, we really want to relieve you of the burden of taking us to school every day."

"As soon as possible," I add. "Posthaste." We watched a lot of *Masterpiece* over the summer. "Like tomorrow?"

"Very funny, girls. Do you remember the route?"

"C to the G," I say.

"And the transfer happens at Hoyt-Schermerhorn," adds Naomi E.

"We get off at Carroll," I say.

"And we walk straight—no stops, no strangers, no dawdling—to school," finishes Naomi E.

"Hmph," says Momma, nodding. "Very good. Did you make your lunches?"

"Yes," Naomi E. and I answer together.

Momma nods. "Great. And Brianna—"

"I made her one too, Momma," I say, holding Brianna's Makeda lunch box out to her. Over the summer, I promised myself I'd do one Responsible Big Sister thing a day, but a lot of times I forget. Since it's the first day of school, it's a good opportunity for a fresh start.

"I'm only eating that sandwich if it has magic in it," says Brianna, trying to balance her lunch box on top of her Makeda backpack.

"There's magic in everything," says Momma, ushering us out of the kitchen. "We just have to look for it."

CHAPTER TWO

Naomi E.

It's normal to be nervous the first day, I remind myself. Especially when you're starting a new school and you didn't get enough time in the bathroom to make your hair look not-slept-on. I might even believe myself if Naomi Marie wasn't looking like the World's Most Confident Sixth Grader, taking long strides right next to her mother while I try to keep up. We've lived here two months now, but it still doesn't feel like my neighborhood.

I've been trying not to compare, to be my own me, and to use the tools we learned at the Blended Families workshop. It felt like we spent the whole summer going to school, with all the workshops and seminars and potluck dinners, and even though I knew it was important, I was only half listening the whole time. It seemed like school stuff, like how I imagine church might be: people telling you common-sense things about being nice to each other and having respect.

I've always been an only child. First with two parents. Then with one. Now I'm part of a family of five. Being part of such a big family is a huge change. But so far it still feels like Dad and I were added to the Valerie–Naomi Marie–Brianna family. This summer we had more visit-museums-and-libraries days than I've ever had in a whole year! And a lot fewer lounge-around days. Maybe now that school is starting, things will change.

We walk the two long blocks to our subway station. Valerie swipes us both in after Brianna ducks under the turnstile, which is allowed because she's still little.

"They'll probably give you your MetroCards today," Valerie says. "But I'll still meet you right after school."

"Can we meet you at the station?" asks Naomi Marie. "I'm pretty sure middle school parents don't pick up, Momma."

"Until two weeks are up, I will be taking you to the school yard and picking you up from there every day," says Naomi Marie's mother, in a voice that doesn't exactly invite trying to change her mind. I haven't figured out what to call her yet. At the Blended Families workshop, lots of kids came up with "natural-sounding nicknames" like Marm and Mimzi and

Padre. I just smiled and said I was still working on it. I wonder how long I can fake-smile about things like that. Because I can't call her "Momma" like my sisters do—I already have a mother. And nothing else sounds right. Mostly, I don't call her anything, though I've been very aware that Valerie is not the type to not notice something like that.

In case it's not obvious: Nothing is simple. Not anymore.

"I don't think we're going to need two weeks to learn our way to school," I say. "That subway map you gave us is really helpful." Naomi Marie nudges me. Maybe I'm laying it on too thick.

"Nice try, Naomi E.," says Valerie. "And maybe it's *me* who needs to be with *you* these two weeks."

We let two packed trains go by before we squeeze ourselves onto an equally packed one, and we take off our backpacks right away. People who get on crowded trains wearing giant backpacks don't exactly win popularity contests. Brianna has the most stuff, which is pretty funny since it's not like they do anything but play in kindergarten. But she had to bring in paper towels and cleaning supplies along with crayons and glue and the regular stuff. Her list was a lot more fun than mine and Naomi Marie's.

"We had such a boring supply list," Naomi Marie says, and I smile, because sometimes we have these moments of thinking the EXACT SAME THING that feel, well, sisterly.

"I know, right? No more crayons and glue. I love crayons.

Does anyone love protractors?"

"What are you most excited about, Brianna?" Valerie asks.

"Homework!" Brianna says. "I! Will! Get! Homework! Just! Like! The! Naomis!!!"

"Homework in kindergarten?" I ask. Valerie and Naomi Marie turn to me with faces that look surprisingly alike. And that somehow convey DO NOT UPSET BRIANNA ON HER FIRST DAY OF KINDERGARTEN BECAUSE IT WILL GET UGLY. You might think that would be hard to say without words, but no. It's right there on their faces.

Naomi Marie grabs Brianna's hand. "We can sit together at the kitchen table this afternoon to get our homework done," she says.

"And there may be a snack from one of our favorite bakeries," Valerie says.

It feels like my turn, but I just smile. Because this is one of those times when it feels like I'm an extra here. I'm trying not to think about things that make me sad, like how it's the first time since . . . ever that I didn't wake up to banana chocolate chip pancakes on the first day of school. Even after my mother moved out, she was still always there on the first day, "because traditions are important." Lately everything has been about new traditions with my new family.

I'm trying. I'm being positive. And I've already found myself being a little more outgoing—even if it's mostly because this family does A LOT! I have definitely enjoyed visiting almost every Shake Shack in New York City (including the one at Citi Field, though I still don't understand why we had to go to a Mets game).

We transfer at Hoyt-Schermerhorn to the G, which isn't as crowded. We're mostly quiet the rest of the way. Lots of people get out, including a bunch of older kids who make me feel little, like maybe *I* should be carrying a backpack full of glue sticks and crayons.

As we approach the steps to the very large, very brick building, I can't help thinking that every single thing feels like a new beginning. And beginnings can be exciting. But also a tiny bit terrifying.

CHAPTER THREE

Naomi Marie

So much for wanting to be with us, because Momma kisses me and Naomi E. quick and says, "I'm sure you girls don't want me to cramp your style," then practically runs away to take Brianna over to meet her teacher, who is welcoming each of her students with a name tag and a Hello Song.

I want a Hello Song.

"I'm not sure I have enough style to even be cramped," says Naomi E., looking around. Some of the girls are wearing heels!

"Speak for yourself," I say. When she rolls her eyes, I add, "I *know* I don't!"

We stand in the middle of the crowded school yard. the little kids are running around and playing on the jungle gym. The big kids are leaning against things looking like they could be on one of those TV shows Momma won't let me watch. Two of them are KISSING right there on the playground, in front of the principal and everything. A little girl is not having the Hello Song at all; she's crying and holding on to her mom's coat.

All the upper schoolers are ushered into the auditorium, and I get a good look at everyone. Then I wonder if anyone is trying to get a good look at me, so I try to seem smart and cool at the same time. I'm glad that I see brown faces, even more than at my old school, which had changed a lot by the time I was in fifth grade. Just like our old neighborhood used to look "like Sesame Street," my auntie Melanie once said, because we had all kinds of people on our block. But now when I go back and visit Xio, our brown skin looks out of place. And she told me that some of the new moms sent around a petition to ban the Icee man from being too close to the playground.

I see a few hijabs in the auditorium; a little boy with a dastaar runs in and right back out with a WHOA BIG KIDS face that makes me laugh. Another boy who uses a wheelchair is making his way to the front of the auditorium, even though a bunch of people are telling him to go to the back. I see a couple girls who flip their hair around even more than Jenn Harlow did.

We can sit anywhere, so Naomi E. and I slide into some seats toward the back. It is LOUD. There's a bunch of high schoolers directing traffic; I'm too shy to look them in the face, but out of the corner of my eye I see some of them smiling at us in that *awwww how cute* way.

"Whoa," says Naomi E. "It's different when you're not the biggest kids in the school."

"Or the littlest," I say. It makes sense for us to be neither/ nor, not one thing or the other. Everything about my life feels like I'm trying to juggle a bunch of raw eggs and dance at the same time. I look around the auditorium. This is a lot.

"Welcome, sixth grade, and all the new members of the Chisholm family!" calls out a woman standing in front of a bunch of other adults on the stage. I'm guessing she's the principal. And even though she's wearing jeans, she has that "I mean business" look that principals have. She just looks out at us until everyone quiets down. It happens fast.

"Again, welcome. I'm Carla, the principal, and we are happy to have you all as full members of our community. We are ready to treat you with love and respect, and expect the same in return." Except for Tom, I'm not used to calling adults by their first names; I think it might be the one thing about Progressive School that Momma's not that excited about. "As you saw in your Orientation letter, we will start the school year by working on the whole-school Community Project, which helps us get to know each other, and begin the work of conversation, collaboration, and action, which are the cornerstones of every aspect of life here. Our theme for this year is . . . drumroll, please—"

The other adults onstage start stomping their feet. I guess they're teachers, even though they're not being that teacher-y right now. All of us in the audience look at each other, and then we start doing it too. We keep stomping until Carla holds up her hand.

"STRENGTH IN DIVERSITY!" she finishes. And we clap again, but the girl next to me says, "I'm pretty sure my sister told me that was last year's theme." Her friend shrugs. "That's everybody's theme." I wonder if Carla went to a bunch of summer workshops too.

She tells us about the chicken coop in the yard (!!!) and vermicomposting (which I hope doesn't involve rats). And sixth graders will get to be "Community Builders" and "Peer Mediators," which sound like things I should be good at. She doesn't say much about math and grades and ELA and stuff like that, though. I wonder if there's an Honor Roll. Then there are more announcements that I don't really hear because I'm looking around and trying to figure out who reminds me of people at my old school. I don't see a Mikey Chen yet—no boy is tying anyone's shoelaces together or having a burping contest with himself, but I live in hope (NOT).

All of a sudden, Carla shouts "601!" and starts reading off a list of first names. I can't understand the order; it doesn't seem alphabetical because she goes from "Gabrielle" to "Ysaye" to "Jamilah" at one point. I nudge Naomi E. "What did I miss?"

"I don't know," she said. "I was wondering what the bathrooms are going to be like."

We both shudder. I turn to the girl on my other side since she has a sister who went through this already. "What's happening now?"

"Advisory groups," she said. "There are three—601, 602, 603. When you hear your name, go over to the teacher holding up the sign with the right Advisory."

"Thanks," I say, and smile. She smiles back, and I hope that means that I seem new-but-not-clueless. She's white, and wearing purple sneakers, and her T-shirt has red sequins on the sleeves and Live Love Laugh across the front. Her hair is dark brown with some reddish streaks in it.

"Ugh, my mom says I better be in the gifted Advisory," she says, putting her hair up in a ponytail. "Or she will have another talk with Carla."

"I didn't know this school had gifted classes," I say, worried. That's something I should have known.

"Not officially, but you'll know by which other kids are in your class. I can always tell. When my sister started at this school, you had to take a test to get in, but then Carla came and got rid of the test so that . . . um, so that like"—she gives me a sideways glance. "So that more minorities could come." She shrugs. "I guess it's cool. Strength in Diversity, ha-ha."

"What do you mean—" I start, but Naomi E. shushes me, because Carla is still calling out names.

"Naomi," says Carla. Naomi E. and I look at each other. "Naomi," Carla says again, looking around. We both start to stand, and then Carla looks at her paper again. "Oh! I see. Sorry, fam." I did NOT KNOW principals could say "fam." Is that even in the rules? "Naomi Edith Woods, 601." Naomi E.'s face gets really red really fast, and I guess it's because Carla said her middle name. I want to tell her not to worry, I'm pretty sure this school has seen it all when it comes to names, but I just squeeze her hand quick before she walks up to the front. Her teacher has very long brown hair and is dressed more like a regular principal than Carla is.

We get through 601 and 602, so obviously the rest of us sitting in the seats are 603, but Carla calls out our names anyway. Red-sequin girl is still next to me, so we're going to be in the same Advisory; her name turns out to be Jennifer, which gives me pause. Jenn Harlow from my old school ruined that name for me forever. But I'll keep an open mind.

"I guess we're in the same Advisory; that's weird!" she says. "Call me Jen, one *N*."

Weird? And isn't saying "one *N*" the weird thing, since it's not like you pronounce two *N*s?

"Naomi Marie Porter," says Carla, and after I get up to meet our Advisory teacher, whose name is India, Jen whispers to me, "That's cute that you and your friend have the same name. Did you know each other before you got here?"

I nod. "Yeah, pretty much. We're, uh . . . sisters."

Jen raises one eyebrow. "Like, are you adopted?"

I roll my eyes. We've gotten that one before. Maybe Jen isn't that cool. "No."

"Wait . . . are you twins, but like those babies that I saw on the news?"

I know exactly what babies she's talking about, because apparently it's big news when twins are born and one is dark and one is light, which is so dumb. Not the twins, I mean . . . the news.

I just say no and turn toward India, who is leading us back out to the school yard for Part One of our project. I want the teachers at this school to think I'm focused.

"Trey is in this Advisory too. Weird," Jen murmurs. I'm not sure if she's still talking about me or who Trey is, and I don't turn around. Part of me wants to say WHAT'S SO WEIRD, HUH? But then she might call me weirder.

She's still talking. "Wait till I tell my mom."

Now I do turn back to her and try to raise one eyebrow, but they both go up so I probably just look surprised. Last year, Jenn Harlow always made me feel like I was making myself smaller so she could feel bigger. This Jen acts like she's trying to decide who I am for me. And also like her mom is kind of annoying.

As we walk by Carla, I hear her say to a woman who is wearing a tracksuit and a whistle (and I would assume that she is the gym teacher except unlike SOME people named Jen I don't ASSUME), "We have three Thomases this year, and two Naomis too." She sees me and lowers her voice, probably explaining the Naomi "situation."

I've never been a situation. I need to figure out what else I'm going to be at this school, and fast.

In the classroom, the desks are all pushed together into bigger rectangles, and we're free to choose our own seats. I can tell that most of the kids were in the elementary school together, because a lot of them save seats for each other, and start talking and laughing. I try to pick a group that doesn't seem too full of friends who all know each other but isn't one of those tables made up of people who no one wants to sit with. You can always tell. A girl sits next to me who looks like she was going for the same strategy; we smile at each other. Jen from the auditorium comes in, and I almost wave because maybe she wasn't calling me weird, and maybe she didn't say *minorities*, maybe it was *priorities*, which doesn't make sense but . . . Then a boy calls out "Jen!" and she sits with him. When a tall Black boy walks in and a couple of kids call out "Treyyyyy," I look back at Jen, but she's talking and getting her hair French braided by another girl.

India lets us know just by how she stands that she's not here for any *your-name-is-a-country* jokes and that probably all these friend tables are not going to stay that way for long. She smiles a lot, though, and when she asks each of us to say one special thing about ourself during attendance, I feel like I get an extra smile when I say that I am working on creating my own narrative board game with a digital component. (Which is what Julie from my Girls Gaming the System workshop told me to call it. I used to just say "a story game that you could also play online with your friends," but this sounds a lot cooler.)

"Love that! Did you know we have a middle school chapter of Girls Who Code here? Maybe you'll check it out." She moves on to the next person.

I smile. I'm interested, but I like that India didn't try to force me (or "strongly encourage," which is when your mom pretends it's just a suggestion but you know you don't have much of a choice . . . and it usually ends up being fun but you would never tell her that). Maybe I'll go to a meeting, but I won't tell Momma right away; she might ruin it by being all HAPPY.

A boy at my table whose name seems to be Milk raises his hand. He starts talking without waiting for India to say he can.

"I've actually been a member of the middle school

computer science society since I was in fourth grade," he says. He's not looking at me with his eyes, but the whole rest of his body is. "They let advanced people join early."

India just nods and moves on to the next person. I smile, but then I also see Jen and her friend giggling and pointing at Milk, so I'm not sure whose side to be on.

After attendance, India goes into a long explanation of our "Opening Project," which is kind of what Carla already said but with more details and words like *core values* and *courageous*. Finally, she says that it's best to just figure it out by doing it, so we start out with the "Find Someone Who" game. We each get a sheet of orange paper, and India calls out the list. When she gets to "Find Someone Who Has Family in Another Country," a bunch of us end up talking together. "Anyone else from DR?" calls out a girl. One other girl high-fives her, and they both say "Oye." I can't wait to tell Xio when I get home. There was nobody else from her country in our old school. Milk, who's standing next to me, mutters, "This is not a bilingual classroom. What country is DR?"

"The Dominican Republic," I whisper.

And he says, "Oh. They should just say that."

There are two other people with family in Jamaica like me, and one boy named Toussaint who was actually born in Haiti, and Traxler tells him to just go over to the DR people, but Toussaint shakes his head no and so do the DR people. Jen is fooling around, kind of running back and forth saying,

"London! São Paulo! Toronto! Split! San José!"

Milk calls out, "San Jose's in California, not another country."

Jen says in a low voice, "Um, no, Milk. I'm talking about San José in *Costa Rica*. Like, where people go on vacation." She snorts in that *you're-so-stupid* way, and Milk's face turns red. "You are so ignorant of, like, *life*."

I think I want to stay away from both of them.

"What a global classroom we have," India says at the end, even though a lot of people say they don't know anything about anyplace except Brooklyn. India promises that we'll put up a big "Heritage" map so that we can put pins in all our countries. She tells us that we are going to explore places in the city that are connected to different cultures and that we'll go on a neighborhood walk to see what's right in the school's community.

When the "Find Someone Who Likes Pizza" question comes, everyone just runs to the center of the room and laughs, and it turns out that everyone at my table likes pineapple pizza, plus the girl next to me read *Brown Girl Dreaming* six times, just like me.

I'm really, really hoping that I can make my mark at Chisholm. Nobody noticed my pockets yet, though.

I hope Brianna is okay, and I wonder if they will come get me if she starts crying. They might not know that if you make Rahel sing "This Little Light of Mine," Bri always stops crying. They probably don't know that Rahel is inside Bri's backpack, even though there was a strict NO TOYS policy too. I also wonder how Naomi E.'s day is going. Maybe I can convince Momma to take us all to Yumi's first. Sometimes a piece of cake is the best way to ease into a new school. I just thought of that, but it's obviously a universal truth. And it's nice to know I'll have backup—I'm sure Naomi E. will agree.

CHAPTER FOUR

Naomi E.

The teacher leads us up three flights of stairs. This building is huge!

When we reach the fourth floor, the hallways look endless. The bulletin boards have big banners on them:

WELCOME BACK! STRENGTH IN DIVERSITY!
GOOD CHARACTER IS OUR SUPERPOWER!

The areas beneath the giant letters are blank—waiting to be filled up with all the work we'll be doing, I guess.

"I thought it might be nice to meet in the library," the

teacher says. She's really good at walking backward and talking to us at the same time. "There's plenty of room to sit comfortably. It's more informal than our classroom. It's perfect."

We walk into the library, and it really is kind of perfect. There's a whole little-kid section with tiny chairs and shelves of colorful picture books. I think about my best friend, Annie, who's having her first day at the school I would have gone to with her if my whole life hadn't changed in June, when Dad married Valerie. I make myself stop thinking about her, because it's easy to get sucked into an I-wish-everything-didn't-have-to-change swirl, and I really do want to give Chisholm a chance.

We follow the teacher to the left side of the library, where the desks and chairs are larger. I'm raising my hand to ask where we're supposed to sit when all at once, kids start to sit, as though everyone but me heard an announcement that we're playing musical chairs. I happen to be standing next to a beanbag chair, so I drop onto it quickly. I tilt and slide right off, onto the floor, and it feels like everyone is looking at me. Because everyone is looking at me.

I take a deep breath to get through the moment (thanks, Girls Empowerment Workshop, for teaching me that we all have "laugh and learn" moments). I force my shoulders down—they're up near my ears in some kind of permanent shrug.

There's a lot of rustling as people decide where to sit, and I'm realizing I've already screwed up. I thought almost everyone would be new here, like me. But there are little groups of girls talking to each other. Two boys are working on a very involved high five. There are only a few other kids sitting by themselves.

I need something to do with myself, so I grab my backpack and open it.

Shoot. SHOOT. How did a Makeda lunch box end up in my backpack? Brianna will FREAK OUT if she opens her backpack and finds my nothing-like-Makeda polka-dot lunch box. But she won't find out until lunch. Oh, no. Do they have morning snack in kindergarten?

I take a deep breath and walk up to the teacher. "Hi, excuse me," I say. I don't even know her name yet and I'm already asking to leave the room. "I just noticed that I somehow have my sister's lunch box. She's in kindergarten, and I was wondering if I could just run downstairs real quick and give it to her and get mine?"

"Of course," she says. "But what's your name so I can mark you present?"

"I'm Naomi E." I say. "Kindergarten's on the first floor?"

She nods. "There are four, though. Do you know which one she's in?" My brain's completely blank, but then I flash to Brianna singing, "Ms. Helen, Ms. HELEN, MS. HELEN!!!!" when the teacher letter arrived.

"Is there a Ms. Helen?"

The teacher smiles. "Yes. Her room's directly across from the office. Come right back!"

I grab the Makeda lunch box, hoping very, very hard that nobody notices (Makeda! Way to rock middle school!) and walk to the stairs. I speed-walk, knowing I'm in a race against Brianna discovering her missing lunch box.

Across from the office there's a room with a rainbow on the door that says, in different-colored letters, STRENGTH IN DIVERSITY. Chisholm School is *very* into its theme! The door is closed. I don't know if I should knock or what, but I do and open the door at the same time. I'm flooded with . . . feeling, with love for kindergarten, how easy everything was when I was little. The teacher is singing to them, and some kids are joining in: "The more we get together, the happier we'll be."

Brianna spots me, and even though she definitely knows better, she jumps up and races over to me, wrapping her arms around my stomach. "NAOMI E.!! NAOMI E.!!!" And I'm surprised by how good it feels.

"Hey," I say, giving her a quick hug back. "I ended up with your lunch box! So here you go." The teacher is looking at me. I smile and shrug. "Sorry to interrupt. I ended up with my sister's lunch box and—"

"*You're* Brianna's sister?" the teacher asks.

I nod, thinking, *Yes, I know she's black and I'm not.* I feel a weird smile starting when I imagine what Ms. Helen would have said if Brianna had hugged me and screamed, *"White Naomi! White Naomi!"* "Is it okay for her to grab my lunch box for me? It should be in her backpack. I wanted to get it straightened out before morning snack."

As though I unleashed a swarm of bees or something, the kids are all buzzing, "Morning snack?" "I brought grapes!" "I wanted peanut butter." It's still going on when I take my lunch box from Brianna, wave to the teacher, and head back upstairs.

"Thank you for being so quick, Naomi," the teacher says. "All you missed was my introduction. I'm Gwendolyn, your Advisory teacher and science teacher. Please, take a seat."

I walk back to the beanbag, but a smirky boy's sitting there. I look around and nearly faint with full-body relief when a girl with glasses and messy hair points to the empty seat next to her.

Gwendolyn tells us to interview the person next to us. The boy on my left is drawing spiderwebs on his arm in blue Sharpie, and so I am especially grateful that this girl is on my right.

"I'm Naomi E.," I say.

She's been taking off her sweatshirt but now turns to look at me. "What's the *E* for?"

Everyone asks that. It's like calling attention to the thing I least like talking about. "My middle name, but I can't stand it, so let's just skip it. What's your name?"

"Edith," she says.

Oh, no.

Not possible.

"Your name is Edith?" I say.

She nods. "People call me Edie. Why do you use the *E* if you don't like talking about it?"

"I have a sister and her name is Naomi too. Naomi Marie."

"Is she older or younger?"

"Same age," I say.

Edie's eyes bug out. "My grandpa told me there was this wrestler or something who named all his sons George. But I've never heard of sisters with the same name," she says. "Why did your parents do that?"

We're supposed to ask five "getting to know you" questions, and I don't want everything to be about the Two Naomis Show. I say, "It's complicated. So do YOU have brothers or sisters?"

She shakes her head. "Only child. Lots of cousins, though."

If I knew Edie better, I might tell her I still feel like an only child—I guess because I was one for so long—but now I'm an only child with two sisters. I'm pretty sure that would sound strange. "Do you know a lot of kids here?" I ask.

Edie looks around. "Last year Ronak and Alessandra and Alp were in my class," she says, pointing with her chin.

"Do you have a favorite bakery?" I ask.

She looks at me like that's a funny question. Not in my new family. I can picture Naomi Marie standing behind Edie, making a face like it is *so weird* that you think this is a funny question, Edith!

"I like this place called Yumi's," she says.

"I know Yumi's!" And how weird is it that I feel like both of us knowing the same bakery is a pretty good sign that we'll be friends?

CHAPTER FIVE

Naomi Marie

I automatically held my breath when I walked into the cafeteria. I don't love inhaling the aroma of Tater Tots, Clorox, and boiled shoes. But I realized that, surprisingly, Chisholm's cafeteria smells . . . almost fresh. Probably because of the salad bar, which is another thing I never expected. The high school kids who work the salad bar all wear hairnets and gloves, but they still look cool. I've been curious, but haven't gotten salad yet. (What if I get a black bean stuck on my tooth, and no one tells me, like Auntie Vonne at Christmas last year? She thought my cousin Wayne was just really happy, because he couldn't stop laughing every time she opened her mouth.)

"Step right up, folks, and enjoy the fruits of our labor!" says a girl, pointing to where I pick up a bowl and utensils. "Get it—fruits!" She laughs at her own joke while the kids next to her roll their eyes.

"Just keep the line moving," says the boy next to her. "And these are vegetables, so that doesn't even make sense. Leave the bad jokes to Tracey." He looks at me. "Do you have Tracey? You're in sixth, right?"

I guess it's obvious. I stand a little straighter. "Yes, I am. Who's Tracey?"

"Sixth-grade art. Seventh grade dance. Tenth grade math. Oh, wait—you didn't start electives yet. Anyway, if you choose art, be prepared."

"Oh, okay. Prepared for art jokes. Um, thanks." *Awkward.*

"I thought we were keeping the line moving, Jonathan," says the bad-joke girl. "Stop scaring the little kids."

"Do you want romaine or spring mix?" asks Jonathan.

A bunch of other kids are crowding the table now, and Jonathan just dumps some lettuce on my plate, so I guess it's time for me to move on. I try to smile so that they will both remember me and then say hi in the halls so that other kids will see that I know high schoolers.

The boy next to him points to bowls of peppers, carrots, and other stuff. "All grown by the first graders in our plots at Urban Green! Harvested by us tenth graders. Eaten by YOU."

"First graders made this?" I ask him. "Cool."

"Um, yeah, okay, it's 'cool,'" he says, smirking a little. "Are you new?"

"Yeah, sixth grade," I say, trying to sound casual. "I didn't go here for elementary. But my sister does. She's in kidner-garden—I mean *kindergarten*!" Ugh. Talking about losing my cool.

"Welcome!" says the last girl, who's presiding over the salad dressings. "Welcome, and good-bye. Sorry, but we really have to keep the line moving."

I don't see Naomi E. anywhere, which maybe is good so we don't sit together; we're supposed to be "branching out" so that people don't think we're weird sisters. I look around for a girl named Gigi; she's in a few of my classes and seems really nice. Momma says, "Be social! Make friends!" How am I supposed to just "make friends"? These are the questions I can't ask, because I think I'm supposed to just know. Or if I do ask, Momma and Tom will sign us up for a workshop about it.

While I'm trying to look for a corner table that's out of the way but not too DESTINED TO HAVE NO FRIENDS, Jen comes up and taps me on the shoulder.

"We're over there," she says, pointing. "Come on."

I hesitate, and she says, "My group has a lot of fun. I told them about you."

I smile. "Okay. . . . I haven't gotten to meet a lot of people yet."

"Yah, some of us have been here since kindergarten, and then there are new people like you and your . . . sister, and so Carla is always talking about 'mixing it up' at lunchtime. You know, community building and whatever."

I start walking over with her, and she stops. "Oh, did you want to get anything else? You don't have to just have salad, you know. There's regular food too, like pizza and chicken nuggets over there. And everything is free now, so you don't have to worry about people knowing that you're free lunch."

. . .

. . .

She goes on. "So . . . do you want me to wait for you?" She points again. "The table's over there. Maybe I'd better get back. I can save you a seat. Hurry up—lunch is short and we want to go outside too!"

Huh? Free lunch? I don't talk much during lunch, but Jen doesn't even notice. She seems pretty popular; a lot of people join us, and they're all laughing and talking about shows that I don't watch. I notice that all Jen's friends look kind of like her. Long, straight hair with a part down the middle. Crop tops that Momma would never let me wear. Jeans that got ripped before someone bought them. Even though I keep repeating "I'm NYE-omi Marie," Jen introduces me as "Nay-Nay" to her friends, who nod and murmur "Awesome" without even looking at me.

Nay-Nay?

This is not my crowd.

When we get outside, I kind of move away quietly and find a spot along the fence to sit. I take out *Piecing Me Together* and try to look like I couldn't wait to get out here to read alone during recess. Jen reminds me of the character Sam in this book, like how she was nervous about going to a Black neighborhood even though she really didn't know anything about it.

"Oh! I love that book!" says a voice.

I look up, and Gigi's box braids swing down toward me. The day's not over yet.

CHAPTER SIX

Naomi E.

You'd think now that I have so many parents, one of them might have thought to tell me that the first days of sixth grade last three months. At least that's what it feels like.

It's not because we're meeting all our teachers and getting new textbooks or any normal first-week-of-school stuff. It feels like we spent whole days getting to know each other. There's going to be nothing left to learn about the kids in my Advisory! I already know that Pio auditioned for a toilet paper commercial. (He didn't get the part.) Gabby spent the summer with relatives in Spain and came back with seven cavities. Halle goes to a summer camp for kids with stomachaches or something like that. I got to know Edie a little better too, and she seems pretty cool.

On Wednesday she waits for me after our last class. And when we step outside, wow. Being inside all day, except at the end of lunch, it was easy to forget it was summer. But out here it's so sunshiny, and all I want is to get home to my barely better-than-nothing tomato plant. There was no time to plant a garden at our yellow house because we moved in July, and I never knew that moving—really, unpacking— could take so long. But I have one tomato plant in a big terra-cotta pot. And in the backyard, there are some rose- bushes and other plants the house's old owners used to grow. I need to see if that enormous tomato is finally all the way ripe.

But wait. What? Why is my mom here? Talking with Valerie and Brianna? "There's my mom!" blurts out of my mouth with way too much excitement for a sixth grader.

Edie smiles. Then she surprises me by asking, "Which one?" Is that a joke? But she's not laughing. Everyone says I look just like my mom. But I think Edie's just trying to be careful, to say the right thing. And I appreciate it.

"The one with two big bags on her shoulder," I say. Mom's always lugging costumes and fabric. We walk over.

I want to hug my mom, but maybe not so much in front of Edie. Oh, no! I'm about to walk into an I-don't-know-how- to-introduce-Valerie trap. But luckily that's when Naomi

Marie finds us. "This is Edie," I say. "And Edie, this is Naomi Marie, the sister I was telling you about."

I can feel myself bracing. I'm not even sure what for. We don't look like sisters, and it's odd that we have the same name; but it just IS, and people have the weirdest reactions, like we're the latest Nick Jr. show or something. *Two sisters, black and white, with the same name? Tune in for* Two Naomis, *every day, all the time.*

Naomi Marie smiles at Edie.

Edie smiles back and says, "Hi, Naomi Marie." And that's all.

I turn to Brianna and say, "And this is my other sister, who's in kindergarten."

"Is your name Naomi too?" Edie asks, and Brianna thinks that's the funniest thing she's ever heard.

Edie says, "It's really nice to meet you all. I have to go. Bye, three Naomis!"

Brianna starts to correct her but then yells, "Bye! You can call me Naomi–Brianna!"

"Brianna is plenty of name for you," Valerie says.

All around us kids are yelling and running. Ronak and Pio are walking toward the subway, kicking a soccer ball between them, around the people in their way. Without a parent.

"What are you doing here?" I finally ask Mom. We have a funny way of saying this to each other, like on a bad TV show, with a big emphasis on YOU.

"Valerie invited me to join you for first-week roundup."

Now that Edie's gone, I still feel weird about hugging Mom in the school yard, but I do anyway. I'm so happy she's here!

We start walking toward the train. "What's for snack?" Brianna asks.

Valerie stops walking. "You may recall this is *my* first week too. How's it going, Momma? It's been a bit of a mess, thanks for asking."

Mom laughs and Valerie smiles at her. Then she says, "We're going to Yumi's. It's not far from here."

"You-me, you-me, you-me at Yumi's!" Brianna sings. She runs ahead of us, then turns and says, "Question. Can we get anything we want, no matter how big it is?" Her eyes are practically the size of the delicious black-and-white cookies they have at Yumi's. I love those but feel funny ordering them now, like people might think it's a joke or statement about my black-and-white family. It's stupid, but it's easier to just order something else.

Valerie and Naomi Marie catch up to Brianna, and Valerie says, "Order anything you want—within reason."

Mom and I fall in behind the three of them—you can't walk five across down the sidewalk, but it's strange. Or maybe it's not. Naomi Marie and Brianna are with their mom and I'm with mine. And we're all together. Other than when my mom picks me up and drops me off, I don't think this has happened before.

Mom calls out, "Naomi Marie, could you stop a sec?"

What could this be about?

"Let me see that skirt," Mom says with a big, impressed smile. "Wow. Did you do that yourself?"

Naomi Marie nods and says, "I got the idea from a book."

"It looks fantastic," Mom says.

Naomi Marie smiles at both of us, and we all start walking again. I feel a big smile on my face too. Naomi Marie worked so hard on that purple skirt.

When we get to Yumi's, Brianna runs to the cake display. "No whole cakes, Brianna," Valerie says. Brianna sighs but then starts jumping up and down as Digger (we have no idea why this is his name, but it is) brings out a tray of heavy-on-the-frosting cupcakes.

"First-week-of-school special," Digger says. "Two . . ." He looks at each of us, then says, "Or three for the price of one."

"I'm having caramel cake, but thank you," Naomi Marie says.

"I'll have her cupcake," Brianna says.

Mom and I decide to share a chocolate-coffee cupcake and a double-chocolate cookie. "It's not enough chocolate," Mom says, "but it's a start."

Valerie gets two lemon-cranberry scones, which is weird,

and we drag over a chair so we can sit together, squished at one small table. Brianna takes a big bite of her cupcake, and as though no one ever told her not to talk with her mouth full (I know at least four people who have), she goes on and on. I have to say, her first week of kindergarten sounds a lot more exciting than my week was. "We're going to have chicken babies! We get to watch them every day."

"That's really cool," Naomi Marie says. "I mean awesome. Or fun. Ugh, never mind."

"And we're going to make butter. I love butter. But best of all: I HAVE HOMEWORK!"

"Shhhh!" Naomi Marie and I say at the same time, which is doubly bad, as we have a strict no-shhhhing rule. Valerie thinks it's rude.

"That sounds good, Brianna," my mom says. "And Naomi Marie? How was your week?"

The bell tinkles just then as the door opens and my dad walks in. Valerie stands and gives him a kiss. Ew. I think Mom notices and looks away, but maybe I imagined it.

"I got you a scone," Valerie says.

"I get to make butter in school," Brianna says.

"Every day, I hope," Tom says. "Because I like butter on my toast every morning. And what about you two?" Dad asks, looking at Naomi Marie and me. "Hello, Sarah. I'm glad this worked out."

"I thought about bringing banana chocolate chip

pancakes," Mom says. "But first of all, ew, cold pancakes."

"Truth," Naomi Marie says.

"And also I think Naomi and I—Naomi E. and I—will have a breakfast-for-dinner tradition this year."

I squeeze her hand. I'm glad she didn't forget.

CHAPTER SEVEN

Naomi Marie

The parents talk about being FLEXIBLE so much, I should be Jordan Chiles by now. Changing classes sounded like it would be great, but it's mostly been running up and down stairs and still getting a *look* from my teachers when I slide into my seat right after the bell. At home, more changes. Dinner used to be fun. Bri and I used to take turns telling stories about our day, but we'd make one thing up, like *Two Truths and a Lie*, and Momma would have to guess the made-up thing, and we'd play word games, and Momma would tell us about the new books that she'd got. Now we always have to find ways to be a new family; there's no room for the things that my old family actually did.

"We're so excited to try all your home traditions, Naomi E.!" Momma keeps saying. I'm like, *What, eating doughnuts and taking naps?* We're all pretty good at those already. And Momma's always telling us to hurry up so that showers can happen. Five people and one bathroom feels like wayyyyy more than three. It's like how Momma talks about my math homework. "I don't get it," she says, shaking her head. "Numbers haven't changed, but I don't understand this new math at all."

Tonight Momma's really rushing through dinner because she has a conference call, so she just rolls her eyes when Brianna talks about how since we call the adults in our school by their first names, maybe she should do that at home too.

"Naomi E.," says Brianna, holding up a sweet potato fry, "my best friend Kiyomi said that you have nice shoelaces."

"Uh, okay," says Naomi E. "Tell her I said thanks."

"How did she even see your shoelaces?" I ask.

"Remember how I had Bri's lunch by mistake and brought it down to her classroom? Sometimes I see her class in the halls and they say hi. So cute!" She turns to Bri. "Tell your teacher to invite me for snack time." Naomi E. elbows me. "They had about twenty-four boxes of Goldfish crackers in there!"

"Twenty-three," says Brianna. "Dougie forgot to bring his classroom supplies. He cried."

"He looked like a crier." Naomi E. laughs, and looks at me like I'm going to laugh too. I try, but it comes out more like a cough. I'm still not used to Naomi E. acting like . . . another big sister.

"It's pretty amazing how much you're expected to bring to school," says Tom. "Cleaning wipes? Copy paper? Even toilet paper!"

"Gross," I say. "We don't bring that in middle school." I think about the bathrooms on our floor. "But we should."

"That's the reality of our defunded public schools," says Momma, because that's pretty much what she says every time we talk about school. "This year, the PTA is actually paying for the part-time science 'liaison' in our school. We can't say 'teacher' because the PTA can't legally pay a teacher's salary. But that's the only way we'd have any kind of substantial science in the curriculum at all. Think of the schools where the PTA can't come up with those resources."

We all sit and think of those schools for a second.

Momma's not done. "But of course there's plenty of money flowing to and from these companies making money from poorly designed tests that don't help us serve our students." She sighs.

Brianna says, "I played with the K'nect set at Choice Time, and some pieces were missing. Question: Can the PTA buy us a new one?"

Tom smiles. "Don't you have a K'nect set here? Maybe

you can donate it to your classroom."

Momma looks real hopeful. K'nect pieces end up everywhere in this new house too.

Brianna puts her hand on her chin just like Malcolm X in the picture in my room. "I'll consider that." Tom squeezes her shoulders.

"Fair enough," he says, and we all laugh.

"Speaking of fair enough and defundification—" I start.

"'Defundification'? Is that a word?" asks Naomi E.

"It should be," I answer. "Momma, I heard Carla talking about needing parent volunteers to help with grant proposals, and I said you wrote grants all the time."

"Thanks, Naomi Marie," says Momma, not sounding all that thankful.

"Anyway, we get to pick electives—they gave us a list," I say. "I might do Computer Science, or maybe Band. And everyone has to do school service. There's Community Builders, where you work with second-grade classes, and Peer Mediation. One in the fall, one in spring. I want to do Community Builders first."

"Oh yeah," says Naomi E. "And for my elective, I'm thinking of doing Drama Games, or maybe Hydroponic Lab."

"I'm so glad you guys are in this kind of environment," says Momma. "Most schools—"

"And Carla says we can use the things we learn to help

at home and in our communities," I say quickly, before Momma gets back to her Injustice Anywhere Is a Threat to Justice Everywhere talk.

"I'm looking forward to Peer Mediation; I'm doing that first," says Naomi E. "We get to decide the winners and losers of fights during recess!"

Momma raises her eyebrows, and Tom laughs.

"That's one way of putting it," he says.

"What's another?" asks Brianna.

Tom thinks for a minute and says, *"The People's Court?"* and then he and Momma laugh, and Naomi E. and I look at each other because obviously this is another old-people thing that we wouldn't understand.

"On *The Community Court*," says Brianna, "they have a judge and a courtroom." We all stare at her.

"How do you know?" asks Momma.

"I watched it at Aunt Mildred's house," she said. "We watch all the court shows."

Momma frowns, and I bet Aunt Mildred is going to get a call later.

"Dougie says he's going to put his boogers in the butter that we make," says Brianna. "I'm . . . deeply concerned."

Naomi E. snorts and a little bit of water comes out, which makes me laugh hard, and then we're all laughing, and this much laughing in our new house feels good and celebratory and fills me up even though we haven't had dessert yet.

Which I hope we're still having, because I'll never be flexible enough to give up dessert.

Momma comes to tuck us in, and after she sits on Naomi E.'s bed and gives her the "blessing on your head," she comes and stretches out next to me like she always does.

"You're getting so big, I can barely fit anymore," she says, nudging me over.

"No room! No room!" I say, like we're in *Alice in Wonderland*, but I scrunch up more so she can snuggle up next to me.

"Momma?" I say after a minute.

"Naomi Marie?" she answers.

"I might have to find something different to call you now. I'm not sure if Momma sounds too . . . babyish."

"But you *are* my baby!" she says, which is what I knew she was going to say.

"Well . . . let's consider it," I say, smiling.

"Where do you think Bri got that one from?" asks Momma. "She is a trip."

"Momma, are there a lot of poor people at our new school?"

"Poor in financial resources? Or poor in spirit? Because—"

"Momma . . ."

"Okay, okay. Of course, one of the reasons that we wanted you girls to go to this school is because it is racially and economically diverse. We live in a city that's both increasingly diverse and increasingly segregated, especially in the schools."

I jump in quick, because she's off again. "So economically diverse means rich people, poor people . . ."

"And everything in between, which is where we are, if that's what you're asking. As this part of Brooklyn has become more gentrified, your school has made it a mandate to admit a certain percentage of students from different neighborhoods and lower-income families."

"Maybe people don't want everyone all up in their business like that," I say.

"What is this about, Naomi Marie? It's getting late."

I lower my voice. "We talked about gentrification at school," I say. "This girl said that it brings nice things into bad neighborhoods. Then India talked about *terraforming*— she said some people say that's where people come into a community and just change it to what they want and don't respect what's there."

"This is a big topic for another time, honey," says Momma slowly, glancing over at Naomi E.'s bed. "The short version is that gentrification is, in a way, both and more. The negative part of it has a lot to do with people with money and influence moving into neighborhoods, sometimes actively trying to drive longtime residents out. And most often, in my opinion, there is a troubling racial component. Now, sleep." She kisses my forehead.

"So, are we gentrifiers because of"—I whisper—"our

new family? Is that why we moved?"

Momma smiles. "We moved because we couldn't afford our old neighborhood anymore, and because we needed more space."

"Okay, so did we get gentrified out, and now we're gentrifying in?" I ask.

"No more questions, as good as they are," says Momma. "We can't talk all night; we have to be considerate."

If I had my own room, I bet we'd be able to talk longer. If I had a smartphone, I could do a group video chat with Kendall and Amy and Toni from the Blended Families workshop.

I look over in Naomi E.'s direction. If I were white, maybe I wouldn't even have questions.

"It's just . . . remember that time when we were at the library, and . . ." I glance at Naomi E.'s bed again. She always falls asleep fast and deep, but I'm still worried that she'll hear. "Remember that lady who thought you were *her* babysitter?"

Momma's back stiffens. "That ignorant— I mean, I wasn't surprised, because it never ends. But still. The nerve to let those words come out of her mouth."

"This girl at school is kind of like that."

"What?!" Momma sits up.

"Sssh," I whisper. "No, it just . . . she says stuff; it makes me mad. And sad at the same time."

Momma hugs me. "It does that for me too, sweetie pie. All the time."

We lie there for a while. I can hear the low hum of the TV in the living room, where Tom is watching the same sports highlights over and over.

"Do you really want to talk about it some more?" Momma asks. "We can go into the living room. Just a few minutes, though."

I'm tired. "Not right now," I say. "But . . . I do. In private, I guess. Does it really never end?"

Momma adjusts my satin sleep cap. "And I need some time to think about how to answer that, and all these wonderfully complicated questions. Maybe an early-morning walk in the park this weekend?"

"Okay . . . but also—not a workshop, please. Anything but that."

Momma laughs, but her eyes aren't smiling. "We're not the ones who need the workshop." She kisses me good night, and I decide that I'm still going to say Momma, at least at home. Because that's who she is.

CHAPTER EIGHT

Naomi E.

It's still the first week of school and already my schedule with Mom is messed up. She had a work emergency that means she's going to have to work all weekend, so we're getting an extra afternoon. I don't know what a costume-design emergency is, but I always picture a jagged hole in a fancy sequined jacket. Anyway, we made it work—Valerie said, "We will ALWAYS make it work." (And then Dad, always honest, if not exactly hopeful, said, "Or fail to do so.")

So Mom and I are sitting on a blanket on a Thursday afternoon, watching Annie's team play one from Staten Island. Annie's parents needed an extra parent—they have three soccer-playing kids with games at the same time in different places, so we volunteered to be Annie's family today. Why not? Maybe I'll keep spinning new families in all kinds of directions until I have too many to count.

Mom and I are looking at the far side of the field until Annie's teammate fancy-footworks the ball away and starts racing toward us. Mom and I try to pay attention, but neither of us is really a soccer person. I hope it's enough for Annie that we're here.

I accidentally let out a big sigh, which makes Mom laugh. "What?" she asks. "Is there something you want to talk about?"

I hear a cheer and look up and see Annie and her teammates high-fiving and jumping up and down.

"Did Annie score?" Mom asks.

"Maybe," I say. "Her team did." I need to watch closer.

Annie runs by, yelling, "Did you see that assist?"

I grin and give her two thumbs-ups. I need to learn more about soccer so I can be a better friend. (I have been telling myself this for three years.)

"Great assist, Annie," Mom yells out.

The other team almost scores, and a big OH! sounds from the Staten Island people when the ball soars down the hill beyond the goal.

"I think I need an assistant," I say.

"I'm not certain," Mom says, "but I don't think sixth

graders have assistants. Unless that's happening now too. Some sixth graders have nicer phones than me. Maybe they do have assistants."

"They don't," I say. "But it would definitely help."

Mom unzips the little cooler she brought. "Cookie or muffin?" she asks.

"Both?"

She smiles, and I take a chocolate–chocolate chip cookie and a delicious-looking apple-crumb muffin. She gets me.

"Is it school? What's going on?" Mom swirls around—not even pretending to watch the game anymore. She's looking right at me.

"Nothing terrible," I say. "I'm still getting used to a lot of things: school, the yellow house, living with a whole new family." I always worry that saying that will hurt my mom, but I'm looking right at her and she doesn't flinch. "I feel like everyone else knows exactly how to act and what's okay to say but I'm just guessing every time and hoping not to make a fool of myself, or hurt someone's feelings, you know?"

"I'm not sure I do know. Can you give an example?"

"Well, we all do our homework in the kitchen after school. But it makes it hard for me to think, because Brianna will ask a question, or I'll start talking to Naomi Marie, even though she's good about getting her work done. . . . I'm just not used to doing homework like that."

Mom squeezes my hand. I'm so glad she's here. It was

really hard when she was living in Los Angeles. There's no way for your mom to squeeze your hand on Skype.

She lets go and starts running her hand through my hair like she did when I was little. It feels so good. "Some of this is just getting used to a new family," she says. "You've had a lot of change at once. But I'm sure you're not the only kid with a new family and—"

"Definitely not," I say. "I've been to workshops."

"Right. You've been to many workshops." Mom knows, because those workshops cut into our time this summer. We had to change plans all the time so I could learn about blended families and multiracial families and girl power.

"I wish I could spend more time with you," I say. I think that a lot but usually don't say it. And I know Mom's about to remind me why.

Her eyes tear up. "I wish my work lined up better with middle school, with you. But when I'm working two shows at once, with that *Magenta Barbecue* movie happening in November—"

"I know, I know," I say. Because I do. But I also know that in the two families I've lived in, and for most of my cousins and friends, it seems like the mom takes the lead. A lot of times I feel like Dad and I have joined Valerie's family. When we go to the movies together, we can't see PG-13 movies anymore because of Brianna. And my sisters seem to like museums, so Valerie assumes I do too.

A whistle blows. "Game's over already?" Mom asks.

"I think just half," I say, but I watch to see if Annie's getting her things or taking a break. The amount of sports knowledge between Mom and me is truly pathetic.

Since there's nobody else I can talk about this with, I look at Mom and make myself say, "At our school, there's already a lot more work than I'm used to."

Mom nods. "Every year there's a little more, right? What is it, ten minutes of homework for every grade—so do you have, like, an hour's worth?"

I can tell that most nights it will take longer. Today I got this awful feeling in my stomach when I needed to turn the page in my assignment pad, because I have that much—two pages of—homework. I can figure that part out, I'm pretty sure, but I'm panicky about the rest of it. "I think I can get the work done. But Naomi Marie is, like . . . I know she'd ask for extra work if she could. And she's making lists of all the clubs she wants to join and another about clubs she wants to start and I think she's studying for a spelling bee that hasn't even been announced and I worry that that's how Dad and Valerie expect me to be now and I guess I'll join a club, Drama Club sounds cool, but do you think I have to do *everything* like her?"

"I'm pretty sure they just want you to be you. That's all you have to be." She smiles and looks all around. "Oh, it's so good to be here. I love being able to do things like this together."

Am I not saying it right? I know I'm not, because all these different things are related, things about school and me and Naomi Marie. I pick one and try to explain. "So am I supposed to know everything about being me? That sounds dumb. What I mean is, at school they make us talk about our rich diversity and culture and what makes us unique and . . ."

"And?" Mom says. She has no idea where I'm going.

"Well, I don't know what makes me unique, but that's not exactly the problem. In Opening Project, I had to make this family tree that showed where everyone was from. Remember the one I made in fourth grade? You put it on the refrigerator. It was kind of perfect. This one looked like a lopsided bush."

I just sat there, doing nothing, for so long because I didn't know if I was supposed to make one that included everyone or two trees for the family I used to have and the one I have now, which includes Dad and my sisters, Naomi Marie and Brianna, only we're not sisters by blood. How do you show that? We don't share roots. And I couldn't bear to think about the sad little leaf or stick or whatever Mom was, all by herself.

I need to figure this stuff out—everyone at Chisholm is good at talking about it, and I have to do better, know more than I do now.

Something catches Mom's eye. "Look! Look at Annie go!"

Annie's weaving in and out between giant Staten Island

girls, moving so fast, all the way down the field.

"GO, ANNIE!" I scream, happy to be actually watching at the right time.

Mom grabs my upper arm just as Annie kicks it right over the goalie's head and into the goal. "GO, ANNIE!" I scream again. And I promise myself to watch the rest of the game closely.

But first I have one important question that needs answering. "What other food did you bring?" I ask.

CHAPTER NINE

Naomi Marie

At Chisholm, we do a lot of reading and conversation; Xio told me she's already had three tests! We haven't really had one yet, and I'm getting a little worried. I've been making study cards every day just in case.

Today we're doing another *not-really-school* thing, a Neighborhood Walk. We've been talking about where we're from, and community, and we made maps of our neighborhoods. People at this school come from all over Brooklyn! And Milla takes the Staten Island ferry, which means she has to practically get up during the night to be on time.

Jen tells everyone she lives in one of the fancy new

doorman buildings that got built where my old dance studio used to be.

"We have a pool," she says to me. "Do you know how to swim?"

"I'm on the swim team at the Y," I say.

"Oh . . . interesting. I've never been to the Y; my mom says it's not clean." I just look at her. "What happens to your hair in the water?" she asks.

"What do you mean, what happens to it?"

"Today, we're recording our impressions of the school community," says our team leader, Jaira. "And then we'll do some COMPARING and CONTRASTING with our home communities."

I move away from Jen and make a quick sketch of an old-school-looking barbershop with one of those red, white, and blue twirly barber poles out front. When the men inside see me looking, they smile and wave. The one in the chair has almost no hair to be barbered, but that's none of my business. We pass three coffee shops that are all packed with people on laptops. Then we go into a bakery called Mazzola that smells so good. Our assistant team leader, Benjamin, does the five-clap thing to make us stop talking. He's a paraprofessional, and I would not like being called something that seems like it means *almost professional*, but he doesn't seem to care.

"What do you notice, what do you think?" he asks. A

couple of us, including me, raise our hands, but some kids just call out.

"I notice COOKIES," yells this kid next to me named Gruber, making Cookie Monster noises, which is so immature. I slide a little away from him so I'm not guilty by association.

Benjamin doesn't even look at him. I like his style. "Who notices something?"

"I noticed that it says 'Italian' bakery on the sign outside. Why Italian? Isn't a bakery just a bakery?" asks Lauryn.

"There's a Polish bakery in my neighborhood," adds Paulina.

"Do you live in Greenpoint or Williamsburg?" asks Jaira. She's a high school teacher, and her twists are superlong, like my Ava DuVernay doll. Which I'm pretty sure I should never mention in middle school.

"Greenpoint," says Paulina. "How did you know?"

"Let's consider. Are there a lot of Polish people in your community?"

Paulina nods. "Oh, I get it," she says. She looks around. "But this isn't, like, an Italian neighborhood."

"It used to be considered an Italian neighborhood," says Jaira. "What would you consider it now?"

I start to raise my hand, then stop. Do I just say "white people"? I see some Black and Latinx and Asian people sometimes. But it doesn't look like they live here; they're usually rushing to and from the train station. The people who I see walking dogs, picking up the newspapers at their front doors, and sitting in cafés with coffee cups and laptops, just being *comfortable* here, they're usually white.

"That lady at the counter is Dominican," says a boy whose name I forgot.

"How do you know? Did you ask her?" asks Gigi, the girl with the box braids who likes *Piecing Me Together*. I don't know how to go up to her and say *HI, BE MY FRIEND* without actually saying that.

"Only white people live here," says Guillaume.

I look at him. Most white kids like him just don't come out and say "white." I bet he's been to some workshops.

"*Only* white people?" asks Jaira.

I speak up. "I think there are Latinx people too. I hear a lot of Spanish when I walk by the Glassdoor Towers."

"What's Lateen X?" asks Gruber.

Oops, I'm talking workshop talk. I thought this was a workshop-type school.

"Latinx is a gender-neutral alternative to saying *Latino* or *Latina*," says Jaira. A few other kids nod and snap their fingers.

Yeah, this is a workshop-type school.

"What does all this make you wonder about?" asks Jaira. "Ask yourself questions about this community and what you notice as we walk. We'll have a community conversation when we get back to the building."

More people come into the bakery, and I can tell the lady at the counter wants the place to look busy with people actually buying stuff. Jaira sends us outside with Benjamin.

"She's probably getting herself a coffee," says Gruber.

I wonder if Momma and Tom looked for a house here. It would be nice to walk to school. But I wonder if people would just assume I didn't live here, even if I did.

When Jaira comes out, she has a box, and we can tell it's cookies, so everybody starts cheering right there on the sidewalk. But she says we've got more walking and "inquiry work" to do before lunch. There are not that many people out, just some caregivers with strollers. Some look like the parents of the stroller littles, others I'm not so sure. And a couple of tiny old ladies (I can hear Nana say "elders" in my head) walking tiny old dogs. They look kind of mad when they see us, and I wonder if it's because we're not little and cute like kindergartners or if it's because we're taking up a lot of sidewalk space. Or if it's that we're not Italian. I wonder if the old ladies are Italian and if they think it's weird to see this class with so many different kinds of people walking down their streets. But nobody owns streets, and our school is here, so they're our streets too, right? As we walk and wonder, I think about our new yellow house. The family that lived there before us was from Egypt, and they seemed like they really loved their house a lot, but I overheard the mom telling Momma that "things were getting uncomfortable for the kids" at school "in this new climate." In my old neighborhood, I used to sit with Xio on Mrs. Hill-Davis's stoop, and sometimes she would even give us lemonade and muffins. Sometimes it felt just like *Around Our Way on Neighbors' Day,* which is still one of my favorite books ever. There are stoops here, but I'm not sure if I'd sit on them. And I wonder what the old ladies here would say if I did.

Since we've been studying Community, I NOTICE and WONDER about it a lot more. When we're walking home from the subway after school, I notice the sounds. Like, there are a lot of people who own bodegas in my neighborhood, and they speak both Arabic and Spanish. (The bodega cats all say the same thing, though: Pet Me Now! Stop Petting Me Now!) And a lot of old ladies (oops, elders) speak Patois to each other, but they sound kind of British when they go to the organic juice bar. We seem to be the only new people who are actually from New York. Everyone else is from, like, Michigan or Oregon or something.

We drop Bri off at the playground for an after-school playdate with her friend Nef, and I notice most of the caregivers are different kinds of brown, and most of the babies they're with are white. But they're all different ages. (The caregivers, not the babies. The babies are all baby aged.)

"I wonder where those women live," I say to Naomi E.

"What women?" she asks.

"The caregivers. Like some of the ones in the playground. When we went on our Neighborhood Walk, we talked about how a lot of people who work in neighborhoods can't afford to live in them."

"We talked about bus routes," says Naomi E. "Boring bus routes."

"Oh yeah, the cuts, right? We talked about that too, because public transportation is how a lot of people get to work."

"I guess," she says. "I hate the bus. I'm going to work right next to my house when I grow up. Or maybe in my house. Work from home sounds good. Mostly the 'from home' part of that equation."

"I don't know if they have so many choices," I say.

"Who?"

"The *caregivers*, remember?"

"Yeah, who would choose to take care of some of those kids, right?" she says. "The screaming . . ." We walk past a dog walker who is tangled up in his leashes but trying to pretend that he meant to be. We both laugh. "*Caregiver*'s a nice word. It could be parents, grandparents, babysitters . . . anybody."

"Does it feel funny for you now because it used to be you and your dad, and now it's . . . all of us?" I ask.

"Nope," she says so fast that I can tell she's lying. "Why would it be funny?"

"Not funny ha-ha, but . . . just different." Sometimes it's both, and I wish we could talk about that.

"What do you think we're having for dinner?" Naomi E. asks. "Is it our turn to make the vegetables?"

Okay, I get it. Subject changed. I won't say anything if she doesn't. I don't want to look like the complain-y one.

When Naomi E. and I get home, Momma is already there.

"Momma, can we take a walk?" I ask. "We haven't done one in a while."

She looks surprised. "You're right. . . . How much homework do you have?"

"I finished it at school; we had a double period of Advisory," I say. "The schedule is still weird; we haven't started electives or anything yet."

"I didn't finish my homework," says Naomi E. "Just in case anyone's wondering."

Momma looks at me. "Let me go get my bag," she says, raising her eyebrows at me and glancing over at Naomi E. I swallow, because I really need to talk to Momma, but I know what she wants me to do. After she leaves, I turn to Naomi E.

"Um, do you . . . do you want to come?"

Naomi E. looks up at me and smiles, and that smile makes me more glad I asked than worried about whether or not she'll say yes. That smile says that I have to remember to ask more often.

"No, but thanks," she says softly. "I have to get my

homework done." When I don't move, she adds, "And don't give me concerned-sister eyes. It's fine. I think it's cool that you guys do that. And maybe . . . maybe I'll come next time."

"Okay," I say. And we awkward-hug. "The offer stands . . . any time."

"Thanks," she says again, pushing me toward the door. "Just bring me back some cake!"

"Do you really think you have to ask?" I say. "I got you."

"How do you know when someone is racist?"

Momma's about to sip her smoothie, but she stops before the straw hits her mouth.

"Well, honey, I go by . . . if it feels racist, then it's racist." She gives me a hard stare. "Why? Did something happen at school? Is there someone I need to speak to? What happened?"

"No, Momma, not really . . . and why do you sound angry? At me? I didn't do anything."

Momma sighs. "Oh, honey, I'm sorry. I just . . . get anxious. And angry, when it comes to racism. But I'm not angry at you."

We walk and drink our smoothies for a little while. We get to a bench next to a bus stop and both sit down near a man carrying a baby in a front carrier.

"You said 'not really,'" says Momma softly, in her *seriously-I'm-not-angry-sweetie-pie*-gentle voice. I love that voice. "What happened, really?"

I wasn't going to bring this up again, but I realize that this is kind of what Momma is here for. "Sometimes people make comments . . . I don't know. Maybe they don't mean to be mean, but . . ." I'm getting all tied up, and my stomach is starting to hurt. And now *I'm* mad, because I'm not the one who did anything wrong. Like when I went to the store yesterday and the security guard followed me from the minute I walked in and then *still* checked my backpack on the way out. *I* felt ashamed. And I'm pretty sure Jen is all kinds of wrong, just like Jenn Harlow, but I just end up feeling weird and unsure with them, and a little bit sick when they're surprised that I get good grades, and they think of certain countries as only vacation spots, and their moms act like they're scared of my dad when he comes to pick me up from school.

Momma just sits and rubs my shoulders.

"How did you know Tom wasn't . . . I mean . . . not to say he's racist, but . . . what if he forgets, or . . ."

Momma laughs. "I don't think that's something you forget." Then her face gets serious. "But Tom would be the first to say that as a white man in a racist society, he has to remind himself every day to be *anti*racist." She smiles again. "So he's working on it. Always."

"I think some people at my school talk one way because they know they'd get in trouble if they say what they really think, but . . . sometimes it still comes out."

"What do you mean?"

I sigh and watch a pigeon pick at a chicken wing bone, which is probably one of the nastiest things ever. I mean, that's like your cousin, bruh!

"Never mind," I say. "I don't want to talk about it."

"You don't want to talk about it *right now*?" Momma asks, but it's not really a question.

"I promise I'll talk about it later." I stand up and turn my face to the sun. "I just want to keep walking for now."

She stands too and holds out her hand, so I put mine in it as she kisses the top of my head.

"I know, honey," she says. "I know."

CHAPTER TEN

Naomi E.

We've been having All-Family Sunday dinners since we moved into the yellow house, and as traditions go, it's not the worst. (Worst: Dad's First-Weekend-of-the-Month Total Housecleaning. Second Worst: Friday-Night Laundry.)

At first, the name bugged me. Because it's all of *one* family. But Naomi Marie and Brianna's dad's not there and neither is my mom. THAT would be All-Family. But now, like lots of things, I don't really think about what we call it—it's just what happens at the end of the weekend.

Everyone but Dad is hard at work in the kitchen, because All-Family Sunday dinners are an all-hands-on-deck activity.

"Could you wash the lettuce?" I ask Brianna, who's standing between Naomi Marie and me and that's really saying something, because one thing we don't have a lot of is counter space. This kitchen was made for maybe one person to cook in. Not All-Family dinner preparation.

I'm trying to make salad dressing, and I haven't gotten to the big leafy romaine yet. "Brianna? Can you?"

She rolls her eyes at me. She's lucky her mom doesn't see, because Valerie is not a fan of eye rolling. "What do you *want* to do?" I'm still learning how to be a big sister. And really, Naomi Marie is the best teacher. I don't mean that in only a kind way. She knows how to get Brianna to do things she wouldn't normally want to do. Brianna looks at Naomi Marie, who is slicing cucumbers and carrots and trying to figure out what to do with the tomatillos we bought at the farmers' market.

"I want to do those," Brianna says, inching toward the tomatillos.

Naomi Marie hands them over. "Be my guest," she says.

Brianna stops inching and stares at Naomi Marie, trying to figure out why she's so agreeable. It's probably because she hasn't any idea how to turn that papery-covered thing into something that belongs in a salad.

Salad. That's what we were assigned. But they also let us be in charge of dessert. So we bought the ingredients to make apple crisp. It's my mother's recipe, and at first I felt funny about making it without her. It's one of my earliest memories—taking out the yellow children's cookbook she used when she was little and baked with Grandma. It has old stains from cinnamon and vanilla all over the pages. But delicious is delicious, so Naomi Marie and I made it together. Brianna thinks she helped, too, but drying the apples after they've been washed isn't an actual step.

The smell from the oven is hypnotizing and wonderful.

"Almost ready?" Valerie asks.

Dad has been "reading the Sunday paper" (sleeping on the couch). "I'm up," he says, which isn't really a response to Valerie's question. "I don't need long," he says.

It's true. Dad's idea of cooking— Well, no. He doesn't cook. But everyone has to contribute, so he takes his specialty from the freezer—a bag of broccoli in cheese sauce. He puts it in the microwave. Incredibly, Valerie smiles at him like he's pulled a tray of homemade croissants out of the oven, even though she's spent the afternoon making escovitch fish and festival and fried sweet plantains, which are ridiculously delicious, always.

"I'll be right back," I say, and step outside to check on the tomato plant. The best part of my old garden, at my old house, was picking fresh vegetables. Salad is actually delicious when you pick something from the plant and serve it when it's still warm from being outside (after you wash it, of course). I didn't realize how lucky I was, having that little garden. Actually, I kind of did. All I have here is this big planter with a half-dead tomato plant. I miss my old green beans. And the giant zucchinis. Shoot! The last tomato of the season, the one I was hoping was ripe, has fallen into the bottom of the pot and started to rot. Next summer, when I can put in a real garden, seems like an impossibly long time away.

"Okay, who's setting the table?" Dad asks, pretending he's actually part of putting this meal together.

"I'll do it!" Brianna yells, which makes no sense until I look at the cutting board where she was . . . turning tomatillos into something that doesn't look like tomatillos at all.

Brianna charges into the dining room with napkins and silverware. Naomi Marie watches as I stare at what used to be tomatillos. I try to figure out how to clear out the papery part that Brianna sort of cut-mushed along with the more tomatoey part. It's an incredible mess. Naomi Marie starts laughing and so does her mother. Then so do I. And it's one of those perfect times when I really feel like we're a family.

"Hand it over," Valerie says. "I'll figure something out."

When we sit at the table, I remember the part of All-Family Sunday dinner that's always excellent: the food. Everything is delicious, even the broccoli in cheese sauce.

"So are you looking forward to Creative Writing? It's a shame it's the only class you two have together," Valerie says.

Brianna says, "No fair!"

"What's not fair, Brianna?" Dad asks.

"If sisters get to take classes together, then I should be able to take classes with my sisters too."

Valerie laughs.

"We are six grades apart!" Naomi Marie says. "You're not exactly ready for Creative Writing. You can barely write a sentence."

Brianna looks mad. "I can write! I can creative!"

We all just nod. Sometimes agreeing is the best thing you can do.

I thought they'd keep sisters in separate classes, like they did with the Martinez twins through elementary school. I guess middle school's different. Creative Writing was my second choice—I put Band first.

I was kind of surprised it was Naomi Marie's last choice since she's always writing—in her journal—and making lists all the time. She sometimes leaves the lists on the desk where I can't help but see them. The most recent one was about words not to use in school, but they weren't curses or anything. I didn't get it.

"And when do you start Community Builders? I'm sure you're both looking forward to serving the school community," Valerie says, changing the subject. Another thing we all do when Brianna thinks something isn't fair.

"Soon," Naomi Marie says. "I'll be working with second graders."

Valerie beams at her. "You already are a community builder

and leader," she says. "You've always shown initiative—I believe Ms. Starr said you were the youngest patron to ever begin her own library club. Remember Shapes-and-Colors Club?" She looks lit up with pride.

I miss my mom.

The timer beeps. "I'll get that," I say. "The apple crisp is ready."

I grab two pot holders and open the oven. The smell is incredible—a buttery mix of brown sugar and apple and cinnamon and baking magic. Also: that smell practically equals my mother. I'm going to call her tonight and let her know how it tastes.

I put the pan on the stove, and when I walk back into the kitchen, Brianna says, "I should get to be a leader of second graders too."

And everyone laughs. Even Bri.

CHAPTER ELEVEN

Naomi Marie

I like changing classes every period, just like on *Tidwell Academy*. Some periods are double periods, though, so in the beginning of the year I was wondering if we'd leave the room and then come back in, just to keep up the routine. But once I realized what I was wondering, I was glad I didn't say it out loud. If I want to make an impression as a Smart Girl in middle school, things like that are not going to help.

It's not so easy to know what you can and can't say out loud here. Like yesterday I said "yikes" and Rob Watson looked at me funny, so I guess "yikes" is too old-school, but when Genevieve said she was feeling "fragilistic," everyone was all "yup, yup," and head nodding all over the place. And Lisa Trotter cursed in Advisory, way loud; I know India heard. Sometimes I think there's a secret rule book that everyone but me has.

"I sent home the Service Learning program letter last week," India says at the end of Advisory. "It was supposed to be signed by a parent or guardian and returned to me today."

Oops, mine might still be in my backpack. I was so organized and on top of things in elementary school!

I raise my hand. So do a bunch of other people, which makes me feel better. India gives us a look that would normally be one of those *You're-in-middle-school-now-you-have-to-be-responsible* speeches, but with India, the look is all we need.

One thing about middle school is that we have a lot of choices. I put Community Builders as my fall service project. We get to help out in second-grade classrooms, and that seems just little enough that I can be in charge, but not so little that they start crying over random things like Goldfish crackers touching carrot sticks at snack time. We had to write a "mini statement" about what we'll bring to the project. I don't have many opportunities to talk about the challenges of having a little sister, so I do. And since Community Builders' main jobs are to help with book circles and writing stuff, I add how Momma is a school librarian and I play a big part in her work. Then I read it over and change that part to just say that I'm a book lover and have learned a lot from my mom, who is a school librarian.

I got Creative Writing for my elective, though. I put Computer Science first, Band second, Drama Games third, and Creative Writing last. How did I get Creative Writing? What's the point of pretending we have choices if we get our last one, which is not really a choice, because obviously we didn't want it?

I thought about protesting, which is something I have a lot of experience in, but after I saw the look Aunjalique got when she asked why she got her third choice for electives, I decided not to say anything. But then I think that maybe I can make it work for me. It'll be a time to shine. I mean, it's not like I don't love to write; I was even thinking of starting a zine club in our new neighborhood. Naomi E. will be all up in it, once I talk her into it. Anyway, I write all the time, like

    In my home journal
    In my fake *just-in-case-of-snooping-little-sisters* journal
    In the storytellers club at the library
    In the digital storytellers club at the library
    In my head
    In my "family announcements" newsletter
    In my Writer's Notebook that I still keep even though
        Ms. Koshy isn't my teacher anymore
    And in my list notebook.

I had a feeling I wouldn't get Band, because at orientation in August, Momma made a big deal of telling the music teacher about all the instruments I play and he started to get that *I-need-an-escape* look and wrote something down on his notepad, which is Always Bad. Sometimes Momma forgets all her own teacher rules when she's being Momma and not Ms. Porter.

Computer Science would have been great, because I think I have a knack for that stuff ever since Girls Gaming the System. I wish I could still go to meetings, but now that we've moved, it's harder to get to a lot of things, including my dad's, and Shelly Ann's. Sometimes I just want to say, *No, BECAUSE I want to do the things that I already love doing with the people I already know and love especially now when everything feels wacky and weird and off balance.*

Sigh.

I was thinking that maybe I'd be the Smart Computer Girl at this school, since I have experience with GGTS and can talk like I know a lot of stuff about apps and games. Plus I remember when Momma took me and Bri to see the movie *Hidden Figures* three times; it was so cool even though it had that part where that Al Harrison guy (who wasn't even real!) took down the Colored bathroom sign. Momma said that never happened, but it's the way society tries to put us on the sideline of the games we invented. She read us the *Hidden Figures* book so we knew all the things that Katherine

Johnson did for herself. I can picture myself being like a Hidden Figure of digital games. I just have to figure out what we haven't figured out yet.

That girl Gigi is in Creative Writing, and I really want to get to know her better, so that's cool. I still think it's weird that Naomi E. is in the same class too; maybe the school doesn't think of us as real sisters. Sometimes I'm not sure either, and I can't tell if it's because we just became sisters, like, two minutes ago or if it's because we see "life through a different racial lens," which is what we talked about in one of the workshops. Sometimes it feels like both. Like when I told her about Jen's comments and how yes, she did actually touch my hair without asking (I KNOW), Naomi E. just said that Jen is annoying and I shouldn't let it get to me. Then we talked about how we both wanted purple combat boots like Kiranmala in *The Serpent's Secret*.

"What did you get?" whispers Jen. She's always talking to me, even though I try to avoid her. It's hard, because I don't want to seem stuck-up, but I also don't want to encourage her to say stupid stuff. Which she has a habit of doing.

"Creative Writing," I say.

"Oh, that's weird. Did you put Dance first?"

Weird again. I nod just to make her stop talking, and keep my eyes on India so I don't get caught talking.

"I'm in Creative Writing too. My mom says it's pretty advanced. I won a national short story competition last year.

If you need help, I can help you."

I nod again. Jen reaches over, and when I realize that she's about to touch my twists again, I lean away. Not today.

"Your hair is so cool; how do you get it like that?" she asks.

I look at her. "What do you mean?"

"Like it's so fuzzy and soft and crazy looking. Like Medusa. I wish my hair could do that. It's so weird that it just grows out of your head like that!"

"Naomi Marie, Jen, please stay focused," says India with a frown.

"Crazy looking"? "Medusa"? I want to ask her what is so "crazy" about twists and WHY IS EVERYTHING ABOUT ME "SO WEIRD"?

I take a deep breath. I don't want to get in trouble with India. Ignore. Just ignore.

I walk into Creative Writing at the same time as Gigi; Naomi E. is already at a table. We wave and smile at each other; then I see that Gruber is at my table. In between laughing really loud every time someone says the word *period*, he taps the table with his pen. A lot. I'm not the first person to tell him to quit it, but when I do, he acts all dramatic. Then he farts.

"Excuuuuuuse me," he says.

"Today we're going to start with six-word memoirs," says Katherine. "They are like poetry, and you'll be surprised by how much you can say about your life in only six words."

I raise my hand. "I can't write poetry." It's true. Even in fourth grade when Ms. Koshy gave up and handed me one of those word grids that she hated using because she "didn't believe in stifling our creative spirits," I just filled it in with my vocabulary words. I got a hundred on the vocabulary test. I can't write poetry, so I don't. Why waste time doing things I'm bad at when I can just be the best at the things I'm better at?

"I'm not sure what you mean by 'can't,'" says Katherine, raising one eyebrow, and the seventh graders giggle. They know Katherine well already. Electives can be taken by anyone in middle school, and you can repeat if you want, which seems totally opposite to the whole TRY-NEW-THINGS philosophy that is on a lot of posters around the building.

"I mean, um, I don't . . . I'm not good at . . ." I trail off. The things that I used to say in fifth grade don't sound the same now. And I can tell by the way Katherine's other eyebrow rises up to match the height of the first one, I'm not getting away with a vocabulary list.

"This is a good moment to review our community guidelines, folks," says Katherine. I really want to sink into the floor, but I just sit up straighter and try to smile like I wrote the community guidelines. "In this class, in order to grow as writers, we . . ." she trails off, and seventh graders yell out stuff like "try new things" (see?), "listen without prejudice" (yeah, okay), "respectful dialogue" (um, Gruber?), and I get the picture.

"I'll try," I say, and she smiles at me and nods. Thankfully, she moves on. I do not want to make a fool of myself with bad poetry in front of seventh graders.

Katherine puts up her own six-word memoir on the Smart Board. "Write, rewrite; living thankful for revision."

I see an opportunity to redeem myself, so I raise my hand. "It's like you're talking about the writing process . . . and life," I say. Katherine smiles even bigger, and the seventh graders give me snaps, so I can tell it's a good answer. Which I already knew.

We get the rest of the period to work on our own memoirs, and I try to look busy. I keep staring at the Smart Board until I think of something like Katherine's memoir. I hope she doesn't think I'm copying. Katherine walks around the room making suggestions and comments. When she gets to me, she crouches down close.

"How's it going?" she asks.

I almost shrug, but hand her my paper instead. I figure she won't mind my doodles of KrazyKat Wilkins in the margins. He's the cartoon character I made up when I had my Drawing Cartoons for People Who Aren't Allowed to Watch TV Club, and I still draw him when I'm thinking things through.

"'Same old me; whole new world,'" she reads aloud. "I

like that! I would love to see you expand on this thought in your Writer's Notebook. And we'll be stopping a few minutes early to allow for anyone who wants to share their work with the class . . ." She trails off.

"Mmm," I say, trying not to officially agree to anything.

"And look—you *do* write poetry," she says. "This feels like a poem to me!" She's smiling at me in that *Look-at-How-I-Inspired-You* way that teachers sometimes do. And I feel kind of tricked, but I smile back a little. Because she's the teacher, and okay, I guess we can kind of call it poetry. But no way am I sharing this, even for extra credit.

"I actually love to write," I say to Katherine, just so she knows. "It's just that I'm not the best poet."

"Doing *your* best and being *the* best are two different things," she says. "What's more important to you?"

I know what I'm supposed to say, but I'm not going to lie, so I don't say anything. I start writing again.

"You seem like such a school nerd," whispers Gruber after Katherine leaves.

"Whatever," I whisper back. Not the best comeback, but . . . whatever.

Taliyah raises her hand. "Gruber's being annoying," she says, like it's a thing that's been happening her whole life. Katherine just crooks a finger at him, and they go outside.

When they come back a few minutes later, Gruber sits at the one-chair table that every classroom has—kids call it

"The Island"—and turns to stick his tongue out at me. I look over at Gigi, and we share an eye roll and go back to our writing. When I look up again, Naomi E. is looking out the window. I know she hates "personal" assignments like this. She kind of hates assignments, period. I'm used to talking about heritage and culture and history, but when we were in the Blended Siblings: Old Selves into New Identities workshops, she never took the Talking Stick. We joke about the workshops sometimes; I'm starting to wonder what she really thought about all of it. And if she didn't take the Talking Stick because she had nothing to say, or if she thought that what she had to say would be something nobody wanted to hear. Either way, that made me a little sad. I probably talked too much in those workshops. I could relax because there were three other Black girls in my group who were nodding at almost everything I said. I know "misery loves company" doesn't exactly mean that, but during the snack break the four of us got to laugh and compare notes a little.

After what seems like only a few seconds, Katherine rings the tiny chimes on her desk. She tells us that we're doing a "Where I'm from" poem for homework, and at first I'm like *Enough with the poems,* but this one is kind of like a fill-in-the-blanks type of poem so it's not so bad. So far, I mostly like Katherine. She understands that sometimes writing takes a lot of talking first. She gets really excited when we're having class discussions, and she lets us get a little loud and we don't always have to raise our hands. Katherine says that she wants us to "notice and note," and be respectful of each other on our own. But if someone gets too interrupt-y, or if things get too loud, she shuts it down fast. She doesn't even yell; she just holds up her hand and looks at us in this disappointed way. It's worse than yelling. And when it's time for quiet, the only sound we hear is the little electric waterfall that she plugs in.

"What did you write?" asks Jen, suddenly appearing at my side. I turn a little to hide my paper.

"Oh, I'm not trying to copy *you*," she says. "But I was going to say, why don't you try writing it like a rap? That might make it easier."

"Uh . . . ," I say. Huh?

Naomi E. leans across her table. "Jen, can I borrow a pencil?"

Jen slides over to her and offers her one with a pom-pom on top. "I need it back at the end of the period, okay?" she says.

I don't write anything else for the rest of the class.

When the bell rings, I go over to Naomi E. and follow her out. "Did you hear her?" I ask in a low voice. "'Writing it like a rap'?!"

Naomi E. shrugs. "Who cares what Jen says? She's annoying."

I roll my eyes. "She just said rap because I'm Black. Like, does she think she can only talk to me in 'Blackish' or

'Blackanese' or something?"

"Whatever, don't worry about it," says Naomi E. "You'll write something good—you always do." She leaves. I wonder what she'd say if I told her about the Medusa moment. Probably that Jen was trying to give me a compliment? Not worth it.

It's funny, writing a rap would have been a fun thing to try too, but Jen ruined it for me. I sigh. Now I'll have to make it extra, like, Shakespeare-style or something just to prove that I care about other things besides hip-hop. Or not. I don't know. I make my way to science and hope that we stick to the periodic table or something. And I am hoping that Jen leaves me alone, that Gruber will stay on The Island, and that Gigi doesn't think series books are too babyish and loves SuperJenga and Adedayo's latest song, and that I don't say stupid stuff out loud.

CHAPTER TWELVE

Naomi E.

In Creative Writing, I'm glad the kid at Naomi Marie's table, the one next to Gruber, asks a question I might ask if it wasn't too embarrassing: "How many do we have to write?"

"'How many'? 'Have to'?" Katherine asks. "In writing, it's not productive to think in terms of how many anything." People start snapping. I don't get it because she didn't give an answer. I guess we're supposed to magically write the correct amount, because before long, everyone is writing. Well, Gruber's not. He's in the hallway for a chat with Katherine.

I'm not sure I know how to do this assignment, but I don't like the way Katherine uses questions to make the people who ask them sound wrong. Naomi Marie, you can too write poetry. (I'm sure Katherine is actually right about that.) We don't count words, even though counting is a pretty important part of six-word memoirs.

Six words, six words, six words.

I like that one. It reminds me of "Love is love is love is love is love is love is love," from a Tony Awards speech Mom showed me on YouTube. But I have a feeling Katherine won't like it. I cross it out.

I sit back. I think. Across the room, Naomi Marie is busy, her hand moving fast across the paper with that half smile she always gets when she's writing.

School's hard, home's weird, life's tricky.

Not exactly right, but it's hard in just six words.

Two homes, three parents, one me.

Is it Peer Mediation time yet? Today's the first day, and I'm excited!

Big family, new house, little privacy.

Wow. I'm kind of surprised by the truth in that. It's hard not having my own place to be. I always did my homework in the quiet kitchen. And now, most times, everyone's talking and it's hard to concentrate.

But just thinking that makes me feel guilty. Everyone, maybe especially Naomi Marie, who has to share a room with me, must be feeling their own version of this: getting used to what's different.

I should just write easy ones, get a bunch done so when Katherine gets to my table she doesn't see a mostly blank page.

September garden, pumpkins growing, summer ends.

Those last two words are wrong—summer ends the day you step into school. But all of a sudden my brain gets drawn out of this classroom and into thinking about what I'm going to do in my garden next summer. I'm especially missing pumpkins right now. They didn't always ripen, but growing pumpkins takes some skills I may still be developing. Even when the pumpkins rotted before they could be picked, I loved watching them grow. My garden was my quiet, happy place. I still go into the backyard of the yellow house with shears, cut back the rosebushes, trim the ornamental grasses; but it's not the same.

I guess that stupid rotten tomato the other night really depressed me.

All of a sudden, Katherine is next to me. Or maybe she's been there awhile—I was kind of lost in the plants in my head. "Are you stuck?" she asks.

This is what always happens when I have a writing assignment; I spin off into different kinds of thinking. "I'm not stuck, exactly," I say in a quiet voice.

She picks up my paper and reads. All twenty-four of the words I've written. In however long it's been. Which I know is way too long to have only written twenty-four words. (But points for my mad multiplication skills, right?)

She points at the one that reads: *School's hard, home's weird, life's tricky.*

"A lot's packed into those words," she says. "You can use your Writer's Notebook to try to unpack that." I must have a blank look on my face, because she adds, "To explore that in greater depth." I nod, hoping she'll move on. But then Katherine reads out loud: "'Big family, new house, little privacy.'"

Definitely loud enough for Naomi Marie to hear, but I don't know if she's listening. I look over to check—she's still writing, but without that half smile.

"Again, a lot packed into six words, which is, in part, the point of this assignment. But also an indicator that this may be something you want to explore in your Writer's Notebook."

She finally walks away.

That's the thing about writing. You're supposed to be honest and tell your story, but how are you supposed to do that if someone else is reading it? Does that mean you can't write the private stuff? Maybe that's the key. I'll write about things that happen. Not things I feel. Like what about:

Year without a garden, bowls empty.

I like that, actually. It's both—something that happened and, in a way, it's also how I feel.

*** *** ***

"If Harris says we need more training before we start, I might start crying," Ronak says as we walk into the Peer Mediation room. "My dreams have all been about active listening. And open-ended questions. Summarizing facts and feelings. I just can't."

I nod and shake my head. Because, yeah. I agree. But I'm excited about starting.

Harris backs into the room dragging a big box. "Your Peer Mediation T-shirts," he says. A small cheer goes up. "When I call your name, come up to claim your shirt. Then we'll go over the schedule."

Gruber is called first, and he does this stupid dance and bows when he takes the shirt from Harris.

"Okay, Lisa Trotter, you can come up. You too, Naomi E."

We walk up together, and I can't believe how excited I feel. It's a T-shirt. I'm getting a T-shirt. "Here you go," Harris says. It is the brightest yellow ever invented and says in can't-miss-them letters Peer Mediator. It says Keeping the Peace since 2012 on the back. "Naomi E., you can put yours on now, because you're the first to go."

"Me too?" asks Lisa Trotter.

Harris says, "No, today is Naomi E. and Gruber."

I want to sink through my chair, through the floor below, down through every floor and maybe end up in a mud pile beneath the school. Gruber is the only person who makes me feel like *I* need peer mediation. How am I supposed to do it with someone so annoying?

"Just follow my lead," Gruber says.

"Exactly the wrong thing to say," Harris says, and I smile an invisible smile as I pull my shirt on over the one I'm wearing.

"The schedule's posted on the class's website—it's your responsibility to remember when you're on and to remember your shirt on that day," Harris says. "The website will also let you know who the alternate is in case of absence and which teacher is on duty."

Gruber starts cracking up—yes, because of the word *duty*.

"I'm on today," Harris says, "So Naomi E. and Gruber, if you need any assistance, just ask. Remember: you'll eat your lunch quickly, then patrol the school yard during recess. Any questions?"

My hand goes up. "Are we with the same partner each time?"

Harris smiles like he knows why I asked. "No. Once everyone has a turn, we go through a second time and you'll all be teamed with new partners."

Okay. So being partnered with Gruber is a one-time thing, and I just have to get it over with.

I'm taking the last bite of apple when I feel Gruber standing behind me. Or see the slightly disgusted look on Edie's face. "One second," I say. I finish chewing and walk over to the bins and sort my leftover stuff into trash/compost/recycling. "Let's go," I say.

"We should be able to do three today," Gruber says.

"Three peer mediations?"

He nods in this way like he knows everything.

"Let's go outside now," he says. "It stinks in here."

He's not wrong. Fish sticks, beans, and vegetable soup.

We walk over to the playground swings. People seem to be taking turns. I feel like a cop, walking a beat, looking for trouble. But cops probably hope to find peace. I'm kind of hoping for a conflict.

The kids on the handball court are shouting. I point with my chin, and Gruber and I walk over to observe. "I don't play wall ball anymore," he says. "I always won, so it got boring."

Gruber.

"That was definitely out, and it's my turn," says a boy who's waiting to get into the game.

"It was in," says a girl with a tall bun on her head.

"It was out," Gruber says, which is basically everything that peer mediation is NOT supposed to be.

"Do you want some help?" I ask.

The kid with the ball shrugs and says, "Let's do that point over."

"Yeah, okay," the waiting kid says.

Gruber sighs big and loud, obviously annoyed to NOT get to mediate.

I feel the same way. And feeling the same way as Gruber is deeply uncomfortable.

CHAPTER THIRTEEN

Naomi Marie

We have Creative Writing again two days later, and Katherine is very excited about everyone's "Where I'm from" storypoem. A few people read theirs out loud, and I learn that Gigi's parents are from Gabon and that she's lived in every borough except Staten Island.

Katherine says people can also share their six-word memoirs instead.

"You should share," I whisper to Naomi E. "It's like unofficial extra credit."

"Do you think I need extra credit?" she hisses back.

Doesn't everybody? "I just meant—"

"Forget it, sorry," she says. "But no, I'll leave the sharing to you."

I don't share either. Jen is making me second-guess everything I do; I'm always wondering if she's going to say it's "weird" or give me that *look* like I'm pathetic and trying too hard. Katherine looks at me, like she's expecting me to volunteer, but I turn away and hope that she's not disappointed.

When we're done with sharing, she says that the library has offered to display our work on its bulletin board. Gruber falls all over himself to be the one to bring the papers upstairs, but she picks me even though I only raised my hand halfway—to look willing but not eager beaver-y. So far the hardest thing about middle school is worrying about how everything I do looks to other people!

This library is not as good as Momma's but it's still pretty good. I see *Amina's Voice* on the display shelf, and there are four whole sets of the Gaither Sisters trilogy, so this librarian clearly knows what's up. *The Belles* is face out in the Teen section; I really want a poster of that cover. Or even better, a poster of me dressed up like the girl on the cover. There's a photo of Rita Williams-Garcia with a group of kids holding up *Gone Crazy in Alabama*, so that must mean they do author visits here!

"Hey, you need help finding anything?" A guy in a T-shirt that says Clone Club and dark jeans comes over. He looks like he'd be wearing shades if he was not inside a school building where shades are not allowed. The mirror kind.

I look up and remember my library manners. "Yes, thank you. . . . I'm from Katherine's class, and I have these." I hand him the stack of papers. "She said that you were going to display them on the bulletin board outside."

"Oh, yes!" he says. "This is one of my favorite displays of the year!"

So I guess Katherine is really excited about her students' work every year. Which is probably a good thing, but I thought we were special.

"I'm Daisuke, the middle and high school librarian," he says, holding out his hand.

"I'm Naomi Marie." I shake back like Momma taught me, even though it still feels weird. "My mom's a school librarian."

"Oh! You're *Valerie Porter's* daughter," he says, in a voice that makes me stand even straighter and smile bigger. "She's the best. I've heard about you. And your little sister . . ."

"Brianna," I say. "She's in Ms. Helen's class."

"I know Brianna!" he says, smiling.

I want to say *I bet*, but I wouldn't do Brianna like that in public. I try to keep that kind of thing in-house.

"I'd better go back down, but I'd like to put *Rickshaw Girl* on hold if you have it. I'm a Community Builder for Tristan's class. Oh, and maybe some Mya Tibbs books too."

"Sure. I love that program. Over here—we have a special

chapter book section in the Everyone area."

Momma would approve of this kind of high-level organization.

"Getting ready for my first session with my students." I like saying "my students."

"Have fun. What are *you* reading now?" Daisuke asks.

"I just finished *Goodbye Stranger, Betty before X*, and *Alexander Hamilton, Revolutionary*," I say. I kind of want him to know I'm a fast reader, so I add, "Last week was a good week."

"I have a feeling that I'll see a lot of you, Naomi Marie," he says.

I check out *The No. 1 Car Spotter* and *Jada Jones, Rock Star* for Community Builders, and grab two copies of *Camo Girl* for me and Naomi E. . . . We're going to do a Naomis book club—she just doesn't know yet. Since I'm picking the first book, she can pick the next one. I'll suggest *Orphan Island*. She'll love it.

"While you all have been exploring the questions surrounding community and ownership, the second graders have been doing the same as they study buildings, bridges, natural habitats, and more around the city," says India before she dismisses our group from Advisory. There are eight of us who are doing Community Builders, and Gigi is one of them too. We've been having lunch together, and have so much in common! I'm going to invite her over, but I have to talk to Momma first. Also, I almost said *playdate* instead of *hangout* last week, and that would have been reaaalllly embarrassing.

"I love that shirt," Gigi says as we go down the stairs to the elementary school floors. "I'm so jealous you got to see her perform live." I'm wearing my yellow high-tops, blue leggings, a red Adedayo tour shirt, and an adire scarf. I hope I look like I deserve second-grade respect.

"I didn't, actually," I say. "My cousin Wayne won the shirt and two tickets! He sold the tickets to some kids at his school and he got in trouble, so I told him I'd put in a good word for him with Aunt Corinne if he gave me the shirt." Oops, I hope I didn't just make us sound like a family of criminals or something. "I mean, it's not like he does that a lot, he's only sixteen, and my momma—mom—says it's because of TV, but . . ." I close my mouth before it gets even weirder. Gigi doesn't say anything; maybe it's too late. I might have already ruined my one *real-friend* opportunity! Great.

We're at Tristan's classroom before I can say anything else. "Come on in!" she says, smiling. She's always got style. Today she's wearing purple combat boots and cat's-eye-shaped glasses with lots of shiny jewels on the frames. Her jean skirt has patches sewn on, and embroidery; and her shirt says Love Is in the Hair, and it totally is—big curls everywhere!

She's got a cart of books ready, and I make a beeline to the blue rug so I can plop down on one of the giant rainbow pillows. This room is almost as good as ours—we have a poster of Solange Knowles on the wall, so we still win. I look around hopefully, but no snacks. I thought second graders still had snack time, but maybe they make a point of doing it when we're not there.

Two girls come over to me, each holding out a stack of books.

"Uh," I say. "Why don't we start with . . ." I don't want to seem like I'm playing favorites even though I can totally tell which girl is nicer. "I know! Why don't I turn around, then you put everything on the floor, and I'll spin around and close my eyes and point. Whatever I point to, we'll start with that."

"Okay!" says the one who's wearing all baby pink, which is not my favorite color.

"That sounds complicated," says the other girl. I think her name is Waverly. I knew we were sisters in spirit. "But okay."

So that's how I end up reading *Tar Beach*, which was the book that helped me start my fabric collage club when I was little. (We used fabric glue to make mini quilts.)

I look at the "tip sheet" handout that we got to prepare for our session. "So . . . ," I ask. "How does *Tar Beach* make you think in a new or different way?"

"I went to Harlem once," says baby-pink girl, whose name is Emma. "Waverly, have *you* ever been there?"

"My aunt Jeri lives on 135th Street," says Waverly. "She

took me to see the mural by Faith Ringgold in a subway station."

"I saw that too!" I say. "One day I want to start a club that goes to all the subway stations that have art. We'll take pictures and make it into our own art project."

"Can I join?" says Waverly.

"Me too?" says Emma.

"Yes," I say to them both. "But let's talk about *Tar Beach*." I've talked about this book a lot with Momma. "Why do you think Cassie's dad wasn't allowed to join the union?"

Emma shrugs. Waverly just looks at the floor. I remember that sometimes we're just supposed to let the silence be with us for a while, so I don't ask another question right away. After a minute, Waverly looks up.

"Do you think one day we will really be able to fly, like Cassie? In the future, maybe?"

"Maybe," says Emma. "I would fly all the way to my god-mother's house in Southampton. She makes me lobster."

"I would fly to Beijing," says Waverly. "I watched a show about it once." She looks at Emma. "Lobsters are big bugs. And Beijing is in China."

"No they're not, and I know where Beijing is," says Emma. But I can tell she didn't.

"I would fly to . . . to Nairobi, Kenya," I say.

"Kenya's a country in Africa," says Waverly to Emma.

"I know," says Emma. "I went there with my parents."

I'm pretty sure we're supposed to talk about Power and Privilege, but instead we get the globe and point to all the places we'd fly to. Waverly knows a lot of countries. She says they have a big map of the world on the wall in her apartment.

Then Gigi and I join forces to read *Don't Let Auntie Mabel Bless the Table*. We go big, doing voices and acting out the scenes. Waverly, Emma, and Gigi's Reading Buddy, Thomas, all laugh; and they all say the book reminds them of their family. I bet Brianna will grow up to be an Auntie Mabel. She never stops talking. Momma says she's just expressive, but I wish she could do interpretive dance or something sometimes. Waverly reads *Stevie* to us, and I'm so proud. When she's done, Emma picks *Radiant Child*, which is a surprisingly good choice, and me and Gigi find out that we both have Jean-Michel Basquiat T-shirts.

"Let's twin tomorrow!" says Gigi. I guess I didn't ruin things! Yay!

"Yes!" I say, then I feel a twinge of guilt. "Well . . . I have to see if I can find mine, though." I've never twinned with anyone but Xio my whole life. Gigi's smile drops suddenly, and so does my stomach. Friendship is complicated.

We finish up with *Tiny Stitches*, and Emma says that her dad is a surgeon. Then the girls ask us questions about middle school; I forget that I'm supposed to Demonstrate Leadership and Promote Community Building, and I tell them that it's mainly more homework and no snacks. Tristan asks if I'm okay with having two buddies, and I say yes, because what else would I say? As we wave good-bye, I wonder if I've done enough to give myself Honors on the self-assessment rubric that I know we'll have to do when we get back to Advisory. Oh, well. At least it was fun. And I'm pretty sure those girls think I'm cool. Sometimes those grades matter more.

CHAPTER FOURTEEN

Naomi E.

After school we take the train, but we'll be getting off at the stop before ours because Valerie found out that they were doing a Makeda the Marvelous program at our new library. Brianna was practically buzzing with excitement this morning.

We both got seats, but not together. Naomi Marie is reading some novel and I can't stop reliving what happened in Creative Writing today.

The bell rang and I was standing to go when Katherine called, "Naomi E., please stay a minute."

Naomi Marie put out her hands, palms up, asking what

was going on. I had no idea. As I walked toward Katherine's desk, Naomi Marie gave me a firm head shake, like You've got this. But I didn't think I had that (and I was right). It made me nervous that Katherine waited until the room had cleared. On her desk was my "Where I'm from" poem. There were lots of words written in red ink in the margins.

"I wanted to talk to you about your poem. Were you able to spend as much time with this as you wanted?"

I didn't know how to answer, since I wanted to get it done as quickly as possible. I shrugged, but Katherine waited me out. "I didn't have better ideas than what I wrote," I said.

"Sometimes these things take time. I'd like you to try again, to maybe dig deeper. Instead of writing Thanksgiving as a family tradition, maybe try to answer with something more specific to your family. I'm pushing you because I know you are capable of more. Look here." She pointed at the stanza or whatever about growing pumpkins. That was easy to write. And in the margins she wrote YES! And MORE OF THIS!

It hadn't even seemed like I was trying to write well. I was just writing what I knew about growing pumpkins:

Sitting on the train, I pull it out and reread it, careful to keep the red marked-up paper hidden from Naomi Marie's view:

I am from pumpkins,
From baby oval leaves to yellow fruit with starfish arms

Hold-your-breath-and-hope-for-no-rot
Giant setting-sun orange pumpkin, ready for picking.

It was awful. Katherine said, "Naomi E., you can do this. You HAVE done this." She pointed at the paper. "I would like to see a significant revision. Think outside the normal parameters."

My face burned hot with embarrassment as kids from the next period filed in, looking like they knew I was in trouble. "Okay," I said, ready to race out of there. "Will do."

We get off the train where we're supposed to. And of course Valerie's waiting for us out front, looking nervous, but once she spots us, she smiles. Naomi Marie and I are subway pros now, but Valerie still worries.

Brianna practically races into the community room and Valerie follows, looking like she's headed to a painful dentist appointment.

Naomi Marie and I settle in the back room, where there are comfy chairs but very strict no-eating rules. We usually have a snack after school, and my stomach is growling. To the point where Naomi Marie, who isn't even right next to me, keeps giggling.

"I know," I say. "I'm starving."

"Yes," Naomi Marie says. "I am very well aware of that. Are you working on Katherine's homework?"

"Um, yeah," I say. "But . . ."

I stop talking when two older girls walk into the room, looking ready to settle in until they spot us—then they keep walking into the next room.

"What did Katherine need to talk to you about today?" Naomi Marie asks.

I don't want Naomi Marie to know I can't even do a simple assignment. "She wants me to think outside normal parameters." Maybe Naomi Marie will know what that means. And then I remember something. "What did you think about that 'Where I'm from' poem?" She said she couldn't write poetry.

"It was . . . well, I guess it was an interesting way to think outside my normal parameters."

"Is that what Katherine said?"

She nods. "Yep. I asked her if I could write a story instead, but she forced me to try it." She frowns. "Seriously, not my best work. I'll have to do something else to wow her. I want Katherine to know that I'm good at writing."

"She'll know soon enough," I say.

"And I think Jen totally expected me to do some beatboxing with some kind of old-school fat gold chain on."

"Oh my God," I say.

"Yeah. Anyway, let's get this done."

I look at my marked-up poem. I don't get how filling in "product names" and "familiar objects" makes it personal. I hate having to do it all over again. I'll do it later, when

Naomi Marie is talking with her mom or something. I am certain that Naomi Marie has never been asked to redo an assignment because she didn't do a good job. I'm sure she'd be embarrassed for me. And maybe of me.

"I didn't mind the six-word memoirs," I say. "But this is hard. I don't know anything about comics or superheroes or whatever." Our new assignment is to write our origin story, including when we realized we had a superpower. Because Katherine insists we all have a superpower.

"I kind of like this one."

"Not a shock," I say. "So what's your superpower? And how do you even write an origin story?"

"Do you want some help?"

I want to not have to do this homework.

I wish it was tomorrow.

When will I get to eat something? I am so hungry.

"Any chance I can talk you into joining Drama Club with me?" I ask. "I'm definitely joining, but I hate going to first meetings alone. It's so . . . lonely."

"I *knew* you were clubly! Welcome to the club! Ha— get it?" She laughs. "When's the meeting? I might have a conflict, because so many clubs are starting now, and I'm thinking about a few of them. I can't figure out which ones go best with my new sixth-grade self."

Having a new sixth-grade self sounds like you're figuring out how to call attention to yourself. And right now that's the last thing I want. And how does Naomi Marie have time to join all those clubs? How does she get her homework done so fast?

We get back to quiet writing. Or she does. I get back to quiet trying-to-write.

"I want Shelly Ann's," I say. "Or Yumi's."

"Maybe your origin story is about food," Naomi Marie says.

"My superpower is not food," I say.

"Food, food, food. I thought you were doing your homework." Valerie walks into the room and sits in the empty chair between us. "Get your work done. And Naomi Marie, let Naomi E. focus."

"Why aren't you with Brianna?" Naomi Marie asks before I can tell Valerie that it wasn't Naomi Marie. I'm the one who keeps talking. "And maybe *I* need to focus too, Momma."

"You know I love all books. But I've had more Makeda the Marvelous than I can handle. Luckily, Nef's there with his dad, and now they're all playing Makeda Bingo together." She looks at Naomi Marie, then stands to look over her shoulder at what she's writing.

"Privacy, Momma!" she says.

"I'm guessing this isn't math," Valerie says.

I laugh. Math privacy. Super-private equations. "Come on," I say. "That's funny."

They smile politely at me. It makes me miss Annie.

And my mom. "We have to write our origin stories," I tell Valerie.

Her face lights up. "Is it exciting to think about your life in that way? To consider how you became the person you became?"

I think about how I tanked on that "Where I'm from" poem. "I'm not good at writing about who I am. But this is even harder than that. Katherine wants us to reveal our superpower."

Valerie smiles like this is a thrilling new development. "Is it a matter of picking which one, Naomi E.? Because you have many."

I have no idea why that makes my eyes get teary, but it does.

And for some reason the tears make me think, *Oh, no!* I've always talked about it with my mom (eventually) when I didn't do well in school. And I will tell her. But do I have to tell my father's wife, my sisters' mother, my Valerie too? Because if the only student-child she's ever had is Naomi Marie, then she might think having to redo an assignment is as bad as . . . something really, really bad.

Whoops. They're both just looking at me.

Say something. "So is Kryptonite the thing Superman eats to have power? Because maybe I need to eat whatever my own form of Kryptonite is."

"You do need help," Naomi Marie says. "I don't know

anything about Superman, and even I know Kryptonite is not something he eats."

"I'll leave you to finish up," Valerie says. "Naomi Marie, let Naomi E. get her work done."

She has no idea how far I am from finished. "Enjoy Makeda," I say, with a little bit of a mean smile.

"What are you good at?" Naomi Marie is not wasting any time.

"I don't know," I say. "Lying around. I used to be good at keeping weeds out of my garden."

"I don't believe that's all. You're a great baker—that apple crisp was so good."

"Yeah, but you helped," I say.

"Superheroes often have sidekicks," she says. Then she says, "To be clear: I am not your sidekick."

Not exactly news. This assignment was made for Naomi Marie. She's so good at school stuff and knowing-herself stuff. I thought they might have to pry the Talking Stick out of her hands at the Blended Siblings: Old Selves into New Identities workshop.

She pulls a notebook out of her bag and turns through the pages, then motions for me to come have a look.

At the top, it says: Things I Like About Naomi E., and there are lots of entries in list form.

The tears come back.

I can't even believe a list with that name exists. "Thank

you," I say. I wait for her to hand over the list, but I'm not surprised when she doesn't. This isn't math, and I get that it's private, that she's not okay with me reading it. And maybe memorizing it. But still. She wrote that list! Was it because she needed to remind herself of things she likes about me? Maybe, but stop thinking like that.

I still don't know what Kryptonite is, but if it's something that makes you feel good enough about yourself that you can do what you have to do, then maybe that list is my Kryptonite.

(But I have a feeling that's not what Kryptonite is.)

CHAPTER FIFTEEN

Naomi Marie

It's Friday, which means recess is extra wild. Gigi and I walk by Jen and her crew singing "It's Over (and Over Again)" so off-key that I bet Adedayo was in the studio sobbing in despair.

"Did you see the video for 'It's Over'?" Gigi asks. "Adedayo and Airi in one song—it's such a dream team!"

"I KNOW!" I say. "It's soooo good. Like, my best friend from home, Xio, wasn't a big fan at first, but that was just because she didn't know. Once she knew, she started listening to her songs in order and everything." I rub my hands together. "I can't wait for you guys to meet; I know you'll love her."

"She sounds cool," says Gigi quietly.

I'm going to sleep over Xio's tonight, but maybe I shouldn't say that. "I bet Jen wasn't even a fan, like, last week, but now she's just jumping on the bandwagon."

"Jen's pretty annoying," says Gigi. "She's always asking me stupid questions about Africa, like did my parents ride elephants."

"Yes! She is always saying stuff about hip-hop to me, and my hair . . . and she kind of acts like she's giving me props, but it's more like . . ."

"Like you're from another planet or something?"

"Exactly." This feels good. It doesn't change anything about Jen, but at least I feel a little less alone. Even though I think she's trying to help me shake it off, Naomi E. makes me feel like I'm making a big deal out of nothing whenever I complain about Jen. But it is a big deal to me; I thought I was good, and here's this girl trying to change who I am to what she thinks is good—to *terraform* me—and I'm not sure if I'm supposed to be flexible or what.

"Someone should set her straight," says Gigi, rolling her eyes. "But my mom says to just stay focused on my work. I need to keep my record clean for high school." She looks at her phone. "Five more minutes," she says. Her phone is not at all like mine; it looks extremely smart. Like genius level. Maybe if I tell Momma that Gigi has a smartphone . . .

I wonder what Momma would think about me setting

Jen straight. I don't want to mess up my record either, and I definitely don't want Carla to think I'm a troublemaker, but I want to stand up for myself. Strong, but not disrespectful. I want to be like that. Kind of like Teyana on *Idris Thompson, Teen Detective.*

I know we'll watch at least three episodes of *Idris* at Xio's, so maybe she can help me take notes. Maybe if I'm a Teyana, the Jens of the world will back off.

Mrs. Delgado basically hugs me into the apartment. "Nee-mee, we've missed having you around," she says. She is the only person allowed to call me that. When Xio's littlest brother, David, was even littler, he couldn't really say my name right, and somehow it became Neemee. Now he denies it, because he's six and wants to pretend that two and three never happened. I told him that if that were the case, he'd actually be four, but he wasn't feeling me on that.

"Hi, Mrs. Delgado," I say, hugging her back hard. Mr. Delgado is behind her, followed by Ricky, then David, like a family receiving line. Xio pries her mom's arms from me.

"Mom, you're going to squeeze her to nothing," she says. But I don't mind; it feels like home.

"Oooh, what if she became invisible!" says Ricky, poking me. "That would be great!" David giggles. I stick my tongue out at Ricky before I remember to ignore him.

Mr. Delgado squeezes my shoulders and hands me a plate

of doughnuts. "Good to see you, Naomi."

"Naomi MARIE, Daddy," says Xio. "Hello, we're in middle school now."

"And there's that white girl with the same name," says Ricky.

"Do you mean her *sister*, cakehead?" says Xio, pushing him a little, but not hard enough to get in trouble. "Come on, Naomi Marie, let's go to my room."

"Why do they get all the doughnuts?" I hear David whine as we leave the room. "No fair!"

"I'll save you one, Davy," I call out as Xio balances two glasses of lemonade on a tray.

"Thank you, but don't call me Davy," he yells back. "But thank you!"

"Check this out," says Xio as we set our snacks down on a sheet on the floor. Mrs. Delgado is not having any crumbs. Xio points to a new row of posters on her wall. They're all the same guy holding a microphone in different poses. "Dougie Roller is going to be a judge on *Vocalympians!* this season!"

"That should be interesting, since he can't even sing," I say, biting into a cinnamon-coffee crunch. "Did they get him so that the contestants would have someone to connect to?"

"You are hilarious. Not." Xio leans back against her bed. "So how is that school? My friend Tammy says her cousin goes to the high school and they do some weird stuff, like meditation class. And no homework."

"I don't know about the high school," I say, "but sixth grade has homework, and we haven't meditated yet." We do have a Peace Corner in every classroom, but I don't mention that.

"Next time bring your homework. I want to see if we're doing the same stuff," says Xio. "We can study together at the library. I saw Ms. Starr the other day."

"You went to the library?" I raise my eyebrows. "Without me dragging you?"

"Oh, you got jokes," she says. "But she hooked me up over the summer with a new series about these girls who start their own band. I love it."

"Oooh! We can have a book club together! Let me borrow the first book, then I'll give it to Naomi E. and we can all talk about it."

"So how is it going with Naomi E.?" Xio asks. "Is there anything you'd like to explore?"

"Did you go to another workshop?" I ask.

"No, but my favorite vlogger did an episode on 'Caterpillar to Butterfly: Supporting Your BFF through the Metamorphoses of Life.'"

I roll my eyes. "Um, okay. Anyway, it's fine. Sort of. A lot of changes."

"See?" says Xio. "Metamorphoses!" I throw a pillow at her.

"We have a class together, Creative Writing."

118

"I thought they wouldn't put siblings together."

"I know, right? But maybe they don't really think of us as siblings, because I'm Black and she's white. I get a lot of funny looks when people find out we're sisters, and someone always asks if I'm adopted."

Xio rolls her eyes. "There's this one girl at my school who keeps talking to me about how 'we can't get good burritos in the hood anymore.' I'm, like, one, I know you think I'm Mexican, but I'm Dominican; two, don't ever say 'in the hood' again; and three, you just got here, like, last year."

"Is her name Jenn?" I ask, only half-kidding.

"Remember her? She was so annoying."

"I'm reminded every day. There's one at my school. And I mean literally. Her name *is* Jennifer. She's a 'Jen with One *N*.'"

"Ugh! Does she flip her hair?" Xio swings her head around so her curls fly, and we laugh.

"Sometimes she makes these low-key racist comments— at least I think they are. . . . I want to say something to her, but maybe I should just ignore her. She's all fake-nice too."

"I know exactly what you mean. What does Naomi E. think?"

"I don't know if she really notices," I say slowly. "I think she thinks Jen's just annoying, and I should ignore her."

"She must see how wrong it is, though. She has your back, right?"

"Yeah. . . . I think she does, as my sister, you know? But

even though we went to a million workshops over the summer and we talked about RACE in capital letters . . . I don't talk to her about it at home."

"So . . . do you talk at all?" asks Xio. "Because, seriously, your family always talks about Black stuff. Remember when your mom would give us Saturday School? And you would always try to get the lessons from her in advance so you could sound smart?"

"No," I say. "But anyway, *I'm* used to it, but I don't think *she* is. . . . I don't think she and her dad talked about this stuff so much before. Sometimes I wonder if she even remembers that I'm Black."

"Like, 'I don't see color'?" asks Xio. "I don't think she's like that. And your mom would not have married Tom if he was like that, that's for sure."

"Yeah . . . and one day at school, this kid asked me why I wrote *Black* with a capital *B*—"

"Uh-oh," says Xio.

"And when I started to explain, he got mad and called *me* oversensitive. What if I bring this stuff up with Naomi E. and she gets upset? Sometimes she seems like she's about to cry when nothing's happening. I'm not trying to be the one who makes her cry."

"She gets upset, then. So what? I mean, isn't that what being siblings is about? Getting upset ninety percent of the time?"

"Yeah, but then I'll get in trouble for upsetting her while she's adjusting to being part of a new family. I'm supposed to be looking for ways to make her feel comfortable. But sometimes that makes *me* more uncomfortable."

"Hello, you're adjusting too," says Xio. "And she seems pretty comfortable every time I see her. Like, she's all about relaxing."

"Yeah, but I think I'm supposed to be better at it," I say. "And also, she doesn't have her mom around as much as I do. . . . I feel like I have to be careful with her about this stuff. I don't want to make her feel bad. That kid said I was trying to make him feel guilty for something he didn't have anything to do with."

"I can tell it's stressing you out," says Xio. "I think you should talk to her; but either way, you know I have your back, right?"

"Thanks," I say. I take another doughnut and give her half.

"My dad says it might do white people some good to feel a little guilty," says Xio.

I laugh. "Yeah, that's what my dad says too. But . . . does *Tom* say that?" I shrug.

"Yeah, I don't know," answers Xio. "But you can always talk to me. About anything, especially this. I know you have a new house and new school and everything, but we got you, okay? You know my parents mean it when they say this is your second home."

We finish eating, and Xio tells me about her evil science teacher and the assistant principal who farts in his office all day with the door closed so that detention with him is a real punishment. I make a mental note to add something about Xio to my "Where I'm from" storypoem. Even if I'm not handing it in again, I'll know it's there. We let David and Ricky come in, and we all play Uno together, even though David keeps messing up. And it feels so good to be home.

CHAPTER SIXTEEN

Naomi E.

Ahhh, lazy days! Naomi Marie and I are going to Lisa Trotter's paint-your-own pottery birthday later today, so I finally got the lazy Saturday morning I've been hoping for. After Naomi Marie and Brianna left for a morning visit with their dad, I actually fell back asleep! Double ahhh!

I was up late reading *Camo Girl*, a book Naomi Marie wants us both to read. I like it, but we have so much homework that I haven't had time for anything else. She finished it the night she got it. I'll need to renew it at the school library, where renewals aren't exactly allowed, but Daisuke will let me because he knows I'm Naomi Marie's sister.

I take the book into the kitchen and read while eating a bowl of cereal. Ahh. Quiet. I need quiet to read, and when you live with four other people, there isn't that much quiet. Dad wipes down counters while Valerie takes the dishes he put into the dishwasher and places them in a different part of the dishwasher.

I bring my cereal bowl to the sink, rinse it, and put it on the bottom shelf. Valerie must approve, because she looks at me and smiles. "You clearly inherited your spatial relations from your mother. I am grateful for that."

"Me too," I say.

"Hey!" Dad says with a fake-offended voice. Then he looks at his watch and says, "It's a nice day. Let's walk to Liesel's party."

"Lisa," I say. "Lisa Trotter."

I run to my room and grab the gift card I got for her present. I was surprised to be invited—I know Lisa Trotter, a little, from Peer Mediation, but I wouldn't say we're birthday-party-level friends. Not friendly enough to know the perfect thing to get for her present. And then the same thing—Naomi Marie was invited too—they're in the same Advisory, but not exactly friends. Still, we were both happy to be invited!

Dad's right. It's a really nice day. As we leave, I notice this one small pink rose blooming. Flowers are pretty and all, but when you cut them and stick them in a vase, they're nice for

124

a while and then they die. Vegetables serve a purpose. And pumpkins—it's such an accomplishment to grow a pumpkin because they take forever and you have to do everything right. But I've been learning about roses, and they have . . . earned my respect. I need to prune those bushes before winter, but I also need to be armed for battle—they always get me with their evil thorns. My arms look like I live with a house full of angry cats.

"So?" Dad says.

"Just thinking about rosebushes."

"As one does," Dad says, smiling.

"Did you see that it's still blooming? In October?!"

"I'm more interested in talking about you. And school. And how it's going so far."

Hm. Did Mom ask him to do this or was it Valerie? Because I don't remember him ever doing more than signing papers I needed signed. Oh, and once buying some shoes late at night so I'd have a box for a diorama due the next day.

"Why?" I ask. I think about that storypoem. Did Katherine get in touch with my dad?

"Why? Because you're in a new school and I can tell you have a lot more work than you used to and I'm wondering how that's going for you."

Nope. I still think Mom or Valerie is behind this. But okay. "It's fine. You know, school."

"Right. And you're getting all your work done?"

Has he been spying? Did Naomi Marie find out I was late handing in my math? "I was a little late with something, but it's no big deal. I don't even like to think about school on the weekend, you know? Time for a break?"

I can tell he wants to talk more about it, but I'm glad he lets it go. When we reach the pottery place, I peek around. I hope Naomi Marie is here, because I'm not sure I know any of Lisa Trotter's other friends.

The birthday girl is right next to an older version of herself, who must be her mother, who's saying, "Okay, parents pick up at three," even though it was on the invitation.

"Bye, Dad!" I say. "Hi, Lisa Trotter. Happy birthday! Thanks for inviting me!" I hand her the gift card and she smiles. "Hey, Naomi E.! We're going to start in, like, five minutes," she says. "You can go wait in the party room."

I walk to the back and see some other kids from Peer Mediation: Sawyer, Sayantani, Ronak. The walls are lined with really pretty bowls, plates, banks—they do not look like they were painted by kids. The party room person explains that we can choose one thing off the bottom two shelves to paint. Naomi Marie comes into the room and asks me, "Do you have your eye on that ceramic doughnut?"

My jaw drops. "There's a ceramic doughnut?"

"I think that's what it was. Maybe it was a wheel. Hard to tell when it's not painted."

"True," I say. I'm so glad she's here.

We go together to pick what we're going to paint. I make up my mind pretty quickly when I see a tiny planter and saucer. If it comes out great, I could give it to Mom for her birthday next month, planted with basil, her favorite herb. Which would be an over-the-top thoughtful gift because the smell of basil makes me gag.

Naomi Marie is still picking her piece when I'm picking out colors for the glaze. I walk over to her. "I can't choose between the mug, which I could use for hot chocolate and it's bigger than our mugs at home so that might be really smart, or this vase, which I could keep my good colored pencils in."

I make my face get as serious as I can. "What on earth are you going to do?" She smiles and reaches for the mug.

Lisa Trotter is painting a piggy bank shaped like a hamburger, and every time I look at it, I start to laugh. I'm having such a good time! I watch Lisa Trotter use this puffy paint to make sesame seeds on the bun, and I use it to make polka dots along the top rim of the planter and the edge of the saucer.

When we've finished, we have pizza, one of the world's best foods, and then cupcakes. "Lisa Trotter!" Naomi Marie says as she reaches for one of the double-chocolate ones. "Are these from Shelly Ann's?"

Lisa Trotter smiles—can't talk with a mouthful of cupcake—and nods.

"Happy birthday to ME!" Naomi Marie says, and everyone laughs.

It's one of those parties where you don't even think about the time, because it's fun and everyone is getting along and eating great food. So it's kind of a surprise when Lisa Trotter's mother calls into the room, "Naomi Marie, your mother's here."

Naomi Marie and I arrived separately, so Lisa Trotter's mother probably didn't realize we'd be leaving together. We both get up and thank Lisa Trotter, tell her how much fun it was, and wave good-bye to everyone else.

We're talking about when we'll get our planter and mug when Lisa Trotter's mother spots me. "Oh, sorry, Naomi E., I meant Naomi Marie. Her mother's here. Yours isn't."

I open my mouth to respond but Valerie beats me to it. "I'm here for both girls."

Lisa Trotter's mother is shaking her head a little, maybe so little she doesn't even know she's doing it.

Valerie's voice is all business now. "Are you ready to go?"

"Naomi E.," Mrs. Trotter says. She looks very uncomfortable and won't meet Valerie's eyes. Then, almost under her breath, she says, "You came with your dad, right? Should I just call him to make sure everything's okay?"

"This is my mother," Naomi Marie says. "And she married Naomi E.'s father."

"Sorry it's confusing," I say.

"We have nothing to apologize for here," Valerie says, her voice cold and hard. "Thank you for having them. Good-bye."

Naomi Marie and Valerie aren't talking as we start walking home, but there's nothing quiet about them. I can feel that they're mad, or maybe hurt, definitely unhappy that they had to explain our family to Lisa Trotter's mother. I wonder if I had something to do with that, if I was supposed to say something I didn't say. Are they upset that they had to point out that we're a family even though we're different colors? I understand why Lisa Trotter's mother was confused. You don't often see sisters with the same name, for starters. And it's not like we look alike. It doesn't seem like a big deal to me, but I know it is to them and I'm trying to understand why.

All the fun of Lisa Trotter's party seems like a really long time ago.

CHAPTER SEVENTEEN

Naomi Marie

Our interim youth group leader is absent, so I have to sit in on the regular church service. We're in the season of Ordinary Time, and the vicar seems to be taking that literally.

Bri offers me a sheet of paper. "Question: Want to color?" she asks, pointing to the tiny markers she's spread out on the pew next to her.

I start to shake my head but change my mind. "Thanks," I say. "Can I have the yellow?"

"I'm using it," she says, putting down the blue and picking up the yellow.

She thinks she's slick, so I just say, "Okay, I'll wait," and she gives it to me right away. I should be a child psychologist!

Momma gives us the *I-know-this-is-boring-but-keep-your-voices-down* look.

I color and make a mental list of things to ask Gigi, like has she read *York*, and did she also ever want a dog like the one in *Ranger in Time* when she was little. I wanted to make Bri be Ranger when she was a toddler, but I got in trouble when Momma found me trying to get her to drink from a bowl of water on the floor.

Finally we sing "Rise Up, O Men of God," which is drier than a Communion wafer, and I think about staying seated, just to be funny, but I'm not messing up my cake possibilities. Still, they shouldn't have sexist songs like that if they want everyone to participate. I'm just saying. I start to mouth the words in protest, then I notice Momma is not even singing, so I just stand and hold the hymnal like her. She winks at me.

We go to Shelly Ann's after church, and she's made whoopie pies in a zillion different flavors and I want one of each, like Oliver Tolliver in the book that Bri used to make me read twenty times a day. And just like Oliver Tolliver, I now know that two is even more fun, so I pick the flavors that Naomi E. would want, like mint chocolate chip and gingersnap, which, coincidentally, I happen to enjoy as well. Woot!

"How's school?" asks Shelly Ann, handing us each a fresh chocolate-zucchini mini muffin.

"It's fun," I say. "There's a lot of stuff you would like, with cooking and sustainability and stuff. And chickens." I don't say the stuff she wouldn't like, like Jen, and Lisa Trotter's mom. I still wish I could take my birthday present back.

"Chickens?"

"Yep, we keep the eggs warm in my class," says Brianna. "With plants and worms and stuff."

I roll my eyes since Momma's busy talking to someone in line. "She's talking about two different things. We have chickens, and we do composting with leftovers from the cafeteria. We grow lettuce and stuff for the salad bar."

"There's still worms," says Brianna.

"Compost," I say. "It's not just worms for no reason." Then she rolls her eyes at me! When I was in kindergarten, I didn't even know what eye rolling was.

"That sounds wonderful," says Shelly Ann. She rings up another customer. "And how's kindergarten, Bri-Bunny?"

Brianna starts hopping. "We share with zest, we welcome guests, we're doing our best to be our best just like all the rest," she sings. "Our learning quest is— Oh, and we have Reading Buddies and two snack times!"

TWO!? Maybe my sixth-grade self should be in kindergarten, for real.

Momma comes over with the woman she was talking to, and it turns out to be Ms. Starr from my library! I hug her hard.

"How are the clubs?" I ask.

"Uh . . . your work remains undisturbed," she says, and I'm not quite sure what that means, but she's smiling.

"Did Momma tell you how we take the subway to school?" On our own, finally. At first Momma was making us text at every stop, even though she tells us not to have our phones out in public. Good thing Naomi E. and me know all about parent logic.

"I heard! So maybe you'll come visit us sometime."

"Definitely," I say. "We have no school tomorrow. I wish the library was going to be open."

'In fourteen hundred ninety-two, Columbus sailed the ocean blue; it was a courageous thing to do, but someone was already here,' sings Brianna. I learned that song in kindergarten too, but now I don't know if it's cool.

"He wasn't that courageous," I say. "Momma, should she even sing that song?"

"Yes, we'll be closed, but our Indigenous People of New York display will be up all year. I got some great new title recommendations from your school librarian," says Ms. Starr. "I told him I'd heard about the Eco-Casita sustainability project your school is considering. It was in our library newsletter."

"Really?" says Momma. "That seems unusual."

"Well, Josh Cranstock also donated a ton of money to the library," says Ms. Starr. "He . . . seems to be doing a lot for the community."

"Or *to* the community," murmurs Momma, frowning. "I thought he wasn't big on public libraries. . . . His money must come with strings attached."

Ms. Starr nods. "One and the same. Strings or no, his money will fund some much-needed technology upgrades . . . but unfortunately, the deal also involves losing the top two floors of our library," says Ms. Starr. "They're going to be converted into a condo development. La Bibliothèque."

"But that only leaves one floor!" I say. "How will you fit everything . . . and everyone?"

"We'll have to make some adjustments," says Ms. Starr. "But without his gift, the branch would have had to close altogether."

"So a gift that means a big payday for him," says Momma.

Ms. Starr smiles that sad smile again. "Well, Naomi Marie, it will probably mean much faster computers, so if you wanted to come back and run that Girls Gaming the System Club . . ."

"Sure," I say, but I'm not so sure. It feels like it's going to be harder to establish my new self AND keep my old one at the same time. Has anyone actually tried Yes, AND in real life? Or is it just another thing adults tell kids to sound adult-y?

"How's Naomi E.?" asks Ms. Starr.

"She's good," I say. "I've been recommending books to her left and right. We've been finding a lot of just-right ones." I want Ms. Starr to be proud of me. I try to stand straighter, but discreetly, like I'm not really trying.

"You look like you got a stick up your booty," says Brianna, giggling. She starts robot-walking in a circle around me.

"You can't say *booty*," I say. "Momma, can she say *booty*?"

"I have to head out, Valerie," says Ms. Starr. She pulls me and Bri into a hug. "Girls, it was lovely to see you. Naomi Marie, I'll see you soon, okay?"

"Okay!" I say. "I'll see you soon!" After she leaves, I accidentally on purpose very lightly step on Bri's toe.

"Owwwwwwwwwwww! MOMMMAAAAAA!"

Momma just looks at us, and we both mutter, "Sorry."

"If I can't sing the Columbus song, how can I celebrate Dijinus People Day?" asks Bri.

"*In*digenous Peoples Day," I say slowly. "And I'll read to you. I think you're ready for *The Birchbark House*." Sometimes I get a little jab in my stomach if Bri asks Naomi E. to read to her. I mean, it's a good thing to share the joy of *Makeda in Outer Space* with someone else, but . . . reading to Bri has always been a special time for the two of us. I'm a little hurt that Naomi E. seems to be a fine substitute.

"Yay!!!" says Bri, skipping around me. "You don't have a stick anymore. But you still have a booty!" she laughs and laughs at her *not-making-any-sense* joke. Momma sighs.

I show enormous maturity and just take the box of whoopie pies from Shelly Ann. "Thank you! See you soon!"

I say. I have never actually said her name. I know I'm not supposed to just say Shelly Ann, because she's an elder and Progressive School rules don't apply to regular adults. But she never officially said to call her Auntie. I keep forgetting to ask Momma. Another thing for me to be not sure about.

I hope we have Youth Group next week. The combination of Shelly Ann's and Ms. Starr almost made up for sitting through service, though. On the train home, I wonder if they left out most of the young Jesus parts of the Bible on purpose. Maybe even Jesus had a hard time in middle school. There are all these stories in the Bible about how those olden-days people never believed Him, and they thought He was just like Joseph's regular old carpenter son, even when He was turning water into wine and walking in the air right in front of them. Maybe that's just how it's always been when you're Brown. People see and judge and decide, no matter what you do. Maybe I'm going to have to decide for myself.

CHAPTER EIGHTEEN

Naomi E.

Saturday night at Mom's was so perfect, which was kind of surprising, because it wasn't like we did fun things. She had a design she needed to make "floatier," whatever that means. And I had some science and Creative Writing homework to finish, because Valerie and Dad agreed on a no-Sunday-night-homework rule. I'm pretty sure that's just Valerie, because Dad never cared when I did my homework. And I should probably take some of the blame, because they made that rule after a really hard Sunday night when I was up past midnight trying to finish yet another Creative Writing revision.

But sitting there, with Mom doing her work and me doing mine, it just felt so . . . good. And I got it all done faster because it was quiet and I could focus.

We stayed up late watching *Roman Holiday*, an old Audrey Hepburn movie that Edith Head did the costumes for. I fell asleep on the couch, and that's where I wake up now.

"Hungry?" Mom calls out. If she had her own superpower assignment, she could write about her ability to know when I wake up no matter where she is.

"Always," I say.

"Myla told me about this place I want to try, Disorder Doughnuts."

Mom's apartment is small—I usually sleep on the bed and she sleeps on the couch—but she has two drawers in the dresser that are mine. I keep clothes here so I don't have to haul them back and forth—usually I just bring my backpack. While I remember, I put all the books and homework in it and zip it up. I've left homework at Mom's before, and Gwendolyn wasn't exactly understanding.

We get dressed quickly and step outside. The clouds look like Pixar clouds, small and puffy against Crayola-sky blue. And I'm with my mom. Whenever I'm with her, I feel this feeling that's a lot like a deep sigh. There really was a big hole in me when she was in California—it felt like I couldn't ever get a satisfying breath.

The doughnut place is farther than I thought, but it's nice

to be with my mom after the long week. It's such a nice day, and a few sugar maples are already turning orange, which is way too soon but still pretty.

When we finally get there, a line is leading out the door and partway down the sidewalk.

"Oh, good, a line," Mom says. "I always love the opportunity to stand still." Which is funny, because she cannot stand still. I got all my lazy genes from Dad. "And it's even more enjoyable when I'm hungry," she adds.

"We can go someplace else," I say.

A short lady wearing a fancy hat with a red flower says, "These are worth waiting for if you have the time." I don't even mind that she was listening in, because she had helpful-for-making-a-decision information. My mouth is watering, and the smell—that sweet glaze-y doughnut smell—makes the decision clear. We walk to the back of the line.

"How's Peer Mediation going?" Mom asks.

We lean against the building, facing out toward the street.

"It's been . . . interesting," I say. "I thought it was going to be kind of fun and it's not, but maybe that's because I was paired with the most annoying kid. It might get better."

"And what about the things you like? Did Drama Club start?"

"Yeah," I say. "We haven't done anything yet, but I'm the only sixth grader who's interested in set and costume design. And I never knew a school could have a chicken coop. It's not a sixth-grade thing, but we all see—and hear—the chickens all the time."

"Chickens!" Mom says.

The line suddenly moves a lot. I wonder if a family of twelve just had its order filled. I wonder if they took all the best doughnuts.

"I started Creative Writing," I say.

"Do you like it?"

It practically tumbles out of me. "I had to redo an assignment, this sort of fill-in-the-blanks poem, and I didn't tell Dad or Valerie because Naomi Marie is, like, a real writer. But there's also this thing where Katherine, the teacher, wants us to write about ourselves, and I don't get how you're supposed to write in an honest way if you know someone else is going to read it. That would make me nice-up my feelings or something, you know?"

"I've learned that it's best not to think about other people when you're creating something, but I understand what you're saying." She smiles in a gentle way that makes me know she understands exactly what I'm saying. "Do you always have to share with the class?"

"It wasn't even ME sharing. The teacher was at my desk and she read something out loud and it was . . . private. And Naomi Marie's in my class and I think she heard, but . . ."

She waits a long time for me to finish. But I don't.

"What?" she says.

"I'm not sure Naomi Marie would want to hear some of the things I write, like getting used to living with so many people—"

"She's going through the same thing, isn't she?"

A dad and son walk by us, both with doughnuts in both hands. My kind of people.

"I think it's different—she's still with her mom, which . . ."

There's no way to finish that sentence without saying something to make Mom feel bad. But she's good at this. She points the way out. "I get the sense that Valerie—and Naomi Marie—are very open to talking about things."

"That's for sure. But Naomi Marie's been talking to her mother forever. They know what's okay to say to each other."

We finally step inside the building, and the smell is insane—so many things: sweet, cinnamon, I think nutmeg (my favorite), and . . . is that bacon?

"But there's always this weird thing. . . . Here, this is a good example. You know how I went to Lisa Trotter's party yesterday? And when Valerie came to pick us both up, Lisa Trotter's mother thought she was only there for Naomi Marie. And it made Valerie and Naomi Marie mad, like just because we don't look alike doesn't mean we can't be in the same family. But I understand why it was confusing. I think Naomi Marie thought it was all about color, but I wasn't sure it was."

The people in front of us are paying. Oh my gosh, how

many can I order, because choosing is not possible. There isn't one I don't want. Yes, there is, that coconut one. But I want all the rest.

"You should really try to talk with Naomi Marie about that," Mom says. "I would guess she has had to deal with that kind of thing repeatedly and that it takes its toll, but I don't want to speak for her. Ask her. Let her speak for herself."

I know Mom's right. Why does that feel so hard to do? I have to stop feeling scared to ask. Outside of those summer workshops, we haven't talked about that kind of thing. It would feel so awkward and forced to try, but maybe I should.

The answer to the question is Three, by the way. We each order three doughnuts for ourselves and eat one right away, and bring the rest back to eat later. And another six for me to bring to All-Family Sunday dinner.

And they were totally worth waiting for.

CHAPTER NINETEEN

Naomi Marie

Gigi and I are heading to Community Builders, and I spot Gruber's dad by Carla's office; he's standing on a scooter and wearing a too-small red T-shirt and a fedora. I think that explains a lot about why Gruber is the way he is.

When we get to class, Tristan asks us to help hang up the class's sketches of the mobile science lab on the bulletin board outside. Gigi and I stand on stools, and Emma and Waverly hand up the sketches. Some of the kids have imagined it looking like a rocket or a pirate ship, and there's one that I think is a hot-air balloon.

"Are you guys excited about the lab?" Gigi asks Waverly and Emma.

"Yep," says Emma.

Waverly hands me a drawing. "That one's mine."

She's pretty good! "I like the way you've used so many colors," I say. That's the way we were taught to praise in our training sessions.

"When I go outside in my neighborhood, it's mostly gray," says Waverly. "I like bright colors. I love trees. That's why I like going to Prospect Park and Central Park."

"Don't you have trees on your block?" asks Emma. "My block won the Greenest Block in Brooklyn last year. I helped plant a lot of flowers."

Waverly just shrugs. "My mom said we might make a community garden in the park. But there's no dirt now. It's really an old parking lot."

As I tack up Waverly's artwork, Emma clears her throat. "It's kind of weird to put in all those trees," says Emma. "We're not going to have trees *inside* the lab. That doesn't make sense."

"Um, it's not going to be a rocket either," I snap. Which is probably not how we were trained (okay, definitely not), but this girl is pretty annoying. We finish up in silence and then go back into the room, where everyone is still reading.

"Do we have time for a book?" asks Waverly, holding up *The Alphabet Tree*.

"For that one, sure!" I say.

Emma rolls her eyes and grumbles about reading easy books over and over. I guess she's back to normal.

Gigi and I take turns reading each page. I get to say my favorite line: "They have to *mean* something."

"Ugh, I hate that book," says Emma.

"Why?" I ask. In Community Builders training, we learn that it's important to give others a chance to back up their opinions. Even when their opinions are obviously WRONG.

"Tristan says it's about the power of words, and that's stupid," she says. "If words were so powerful, then why do we say 'Sticks and stones may break my bones but words can never hurt me'?"

"Uh . . . good question," says Gigi, looking at me.

"Um," I say, thinking fast. "It's about context."

"What's 'context'?" asks Waverly.

Emma glares at her. "This is *my* question," she snaps. "What's 'context'?"

"Well, like in sticks and stones it means that the person is saying that if you're calling them mean names or something, they won't let you make them feel bad. They . . . they are using *inside* words to build themselves up from the inside. So the mean words are overpowered by the good ones."

"Like affirmations? When we fill someone's bucket?" asks Waverly.

I nod. "Exactly."

"So if I call Waverly a stupid idiot, it's okay because she has words inside her that tell her she's not a stupid idiot? Even if I say it a hundred times?" asks Emma in the most fake-phony nice voice ever.

Waverly narrows her eyes.

"Good for you, Stupid Idiot Waverly!" Emma laughs. Gigi's Reading Buddy, Thomas, moves a little away from all of us.

"No, Emma, and you know that's not—" I start, but Waverly's got her own back.

"You be quiet!" she yells at Emma. "You're always saying mean things, and they hurt!"

Tristan looks over at us. "Waverly, do you need some quiet time?"

"No!" yells Waverly. Emma just smiles. "No!" Waverly yells again, waving her arm and knocking the book out of my hands by mistake.

"It sounds like you do." Tristan points to the Quiet Corner chair that faces the poster that says Be the Change You Want to See in the World. Waverly folds her arms.

"Tristan," I start, but she holds up her hand. "Thank you, Naomi Marie. I got it from here. Waverly has been having a difficult morning."

"But—"

"*Thank you*, Naomi Marie."

I look at Gigi, and she shrugs, mouthing, *What can we do?*

We know that Emma was the instigator here. I'm supposed to be in charge of both Waverly and Emma, and I think I'm making it worse for Waverly, like there's a spotlight on her or something. Everyone in the class is staring. So I just walk with her over to the Quiet Corner. "Sorry," I whisper. "I know it's not your fault."

Waverly shrugs and turns away from me. I feel like I've let her down.

At the end of the period, Gigi comes with me to tell Tristan the whole story, but she looks like she knows all about the characters and has heard this story before. *But there's a plot twist!* I want to say. She seems a little annoyed and just tells us she'll handle it.

"Bye, Reading Buddies!" says Emma loudly. "Thank you!" I roll my eyes, and Gigi mumbles a bye.

Tristan frowns at us, like we're not being role models. She's probably wondering why she ever let me have one Reading Buddy, let alone two. I want to explain that I don't think we should reward sneaky, bad, fake behavior; but I don't know how. I open my mouth, but Tristan kind of shoos us out and starts a lesson on the construction of the Brooklyn Bridge. Great. I need to read *The Alphabet Tree* again, because I'm having a really hard time putting the right words together these days.

In the old days, Creative Writing would have made me feel better, but it's really not the easy-peasy-lemon-squeezy thing it was in fifth grade. Katherine is that kind of stealth *challenge yourself* teacher too, all smiley but then saying things like "Self is relational. . . . Self is fractured. . . . Language is a part of self, and language in community can vary," and I'm, like, What does that even mean? What happened to Write About Your Summer Vacation, which I used to hate, but I guess I didn't know how good I had it. And now I want Katherine to know how good I am. But I don't want Gruber to say I'm just a school nerd again.

We have to think about all the different groups and "memberships" we have, and "how they intersect and diverge." At least I know how to spell and define these words. Does that mean I'm a word nerd?

I write that down.

Then I add . . .

Black Person

Board Game Lover

Computer Game Lover (but I don't know if I'll keep that there because even though Momma's the one who sent me to GGTS, she's still all restrictive about the computer and video games, and we have NO GAMES on our phones)

Daughter

Book Lover

#BlackGirlMagic? (But maybe I don't have that . . . yet)

Jamaican (but last year, Tyril said I couldn't put that because I was born in New York)

New Yorker

Baker (well, only of two things, but I can make one-bowl chocolate and strawberry cakes!)

Liker of Baked Things

Waffle Maker (like, expert level)

And what about the things people call me, like

Weird

Nerd (not in the good way)

Overachiever

Bossy

I decide to stop there because it's making me sad, and I don't want to add *Crybaby* or something to the list. I wonder if I can include things I want to be. Are those my groups? My memberships? Maybe membership pending?

Runner (I just have to practice)

Tennis player

Naomi E.'s Best Friend (after Annie, and maybe Edie, if she thinks of me that way)

Writer (at least, I thought so)

Middle Schooler

Stylista (I write that down, but I know I'll erase it in case anyone else sees)

Lover of Languages

World Traveler (one day!)

Musician (I need to practice piano more)

Dancer

Big sister

Stepsister (Why is it "step"?)

Should I just say "sister"? That would include both, but I'm different in each sister role. I look over my list and realize that I belong to a lot of different groups! No wonder I'm so confused.

I feel like I'm walking on an invisible tightrope, and I'm not sure if I'm supposed to provide my own net. I thought we'd do stuff in Community Builders like change the bad school rules and tell the little kids to enjoy the fun while they can. So far we've just been reading to them, and we made a "Problem Box" that Tristan said would be kept in the Peace Corner. The kids in her class are supposed to write down "community problems" and put them in the box, then the Community Builders can pick one each week to discuss with the class. It's hard to tell how to get a good grade. (Though wondering about good grades doesn't seem like a thing that would get a good one.) I guess it's all part of "resolving conflicts creatively," but so far, we only got one note about how somebody eats their boogers (we all know who *that* is). What if Waverly and Emma's situation ends up in the Problem Box? I didn't know how to help them when it was just us; what will I do when a whole class of second graders is waiting for me to do something? I think Waverly is already in the Problem Box in a lot of people's opinions. Is she the one who has to change, or do people need to change their minds?

I wonder what would happen if I made a "Problem Box" in our room at home. I could write down all the questions that I want to ask Naomi E., like why doesn't she fold her clothes as soon as they come out of the dryer, does she think Lisa Trotter's mom is a Jen, does she ever want to live with her mom, and does she see me as her Black sister or just her sister or something else. And then she could just write back her answers. Sometimes writing the words makes them a little less scary. But then I wonder: *What answers do I want? And what if she asks me questions back?*

CHAPTER TWENTY

Naomi E.

"Do you think Ronak's late?" I ask Edie in Advisory. I've been watching the door, waiting for him to walk in.

Edie is sneaking bites of a Kind bar because Gwendolyn has a strict no-food-in-the-classroom policy, but Edie never has time for breakfast, I guess, because she's always sneaking bites of something. She puts up her hand to show she needs to finish chewing, then asks, "Why do you care if Ronak's late?"

Valid question. "He's my peer mediation partner today," I say. "And when I was looking at the website last night, I noticed who his substitute is if he's absent."

Edie looks confused, because she hasn't been my friend long enough to know this is exactly the kind of luck I have. But then she gets it—realizes what I'm about to say before I even make the hard G sound in my throat. "No way. Gruber?"

I sigh. And send up a silent prayer for Ronak's health.

At lunch, I'm eating and talking with Edie about the newest, really hard Creative Writing assignment, with words I don't even understand, like *relational* and *fractured*, when Gruber stands behind me. I can practically feel his presence, like some kind of foul, dark shadow. I'd been hoping he wouldn't know he was today's alternate.

"Harris says I have to do peer mediation with you today. Someone's absent."

"Ronak," I say under my breath, feeling kind of mad at Ronak even though he probably didn't choose to get a stomach bug or strep throat or whatever.

I shove the rest of my ham sandwich into my mouth while at the same time putting away everything I didn't eat: carrot sticks, a "fun-size" candy bar from the Halloween bag I opened (and snuck a piece into Naomi Marie's and Brianna's lunch boxes too).

Gruber sighs and loudly taps his foot, then says, "I'm WAITING."

"See you later," I say to Edie. And then to Gruber, "Fine, let's go."

We step outside—it's one of those beautiful, early-fall days, bright sunshine and cool breeze.

Before we've even taken one full lap around the school yard, someone starts tugging on my shirt. "Could you come help?"

"Sure," I say. "What's up?"

"My sister needs some help."

"Then your sister should come see us," Gruber says, which might be true but doesn't sound very helpful.

"Can you take me to her?" I ask. I should probably be talking in plural since peer mediators work in teams, but it's hard to link myself with Gruber, even if it is just link-by-pronoun.

She leads us to a spot against the fence where three girls are sitting, staring at another girl, who's crying. I kneel down and ask, "Do you need some help? I'm one of the peer mediators, and if you want, we can try to help you."

The crier pulls an already-crumpled tissue out of her pocket and wipes her nose.

"Why don't you tell me what happened," I say.

Gruber's just watching. Which I am actually thankful for. I don't think he'd be helpful, or maybe I mean kind, with these . . . I'm guessing third graders.

No need to waste thankfulness on Gruber. "What happened?" he asks in a voice that's not exactly nice.

No one talks.

I look at the crier's sister, the one who found Gruber and me. "Can *you* tell me what happened?" I'm completely forgetting the things we were trained to do. Well, *What happened?* is kind of an open-ended question. But the girl who got us isn't directly involved.

"Elle, that's my sister," she says with a flop of her hand in the crier's direction.

"Just the letter *L*?" Gruber says. (I knew Gruber would say that.)

The crier looks at him. "It's a name," she says, which makes me smile. "We were playing freeze tag and I tagged Mariah, I really did, and she said I didn't and she always does that."

"So she was cheating," Gruber says.

"Hang on," I say. "Can we just talk to Mariah and Elle for a minute?" The other girls nod but don't move, so I motion to Elle and Mariah to follow me to the corner of the school yard. Gruber just stands there until I remind him to come with us.

"Have you done peer mediation before?" I ask the girls.

They both shake their heads. They're working really hard not to look at each other.

"There are some rules," I say, "but it's easy. You'll each get a turn to talk. There's no interrupting, no name-calling. And can we all agree that we'll work together to find a solution?"

They don't respond, so I continue.

"Mariah, why don't you tell me what happened?"

She sighs like this is annoying. "We were playing freeze tag even though I wanted to play blob tag. And Elle was it. She thought she tagged me, but she missed."

"How do you feel about that?" Gruber asks. I do not faint, but I am surprised.

"Annoyed. It's annoying that she's cheating."

"I—"

"I'm sorry, Elle," Gruber says, "but you can't interrupt. You'll get a turn."

Gruber repeats back to Mariah, "So you felt annoyed because she cheated."

"I think it might be fairer to say you felt annoyed because you thought she didn't tag you when she thought she did. Is that right?" I ask.

Mariah shrugs and half nods yes.

"Okay, Elle," I say. "Why don't you tell us your side of the story now."

"I tagged her and she said I didn't. You already know that."

"And how did that make you feel?" I ask.

"Like *crying*. So I *cried*," she says.

"Like she always does," Mariah says.

"No interrupting," Gruber and I say at the same time. (Ew.)

I look up at the sky—not a cloud there. What am I supposed to say next? Oh, right. "Okay, Elle, what do you want from Mariah?"

"To admit I tagged her and for her to be IT. She's *never* IT."

"And Mariah, what do you want from Elle?"

"For her to be IT," she says, a big, fat DUH in her voice.

"Mariah, can you think of a fair solution?"

"For her to be IT."

"Other than that. Can you think of some compromise?"
Mariah shrugs.

"How about you, Elle?" I ask. "Can you think of a fair solution?"

"For her to be IT," she says, "since I tagged her and she knows it. She always gets her way, and it's not fair."

Gruber gives me a look. "What do we do?" he asks.

What a shock. Gruber doesn't remember the resolution technique Harris said would work when all else failed.

"If we can't come up with a solution, we can try rock/paper/scissors," I say. "Whoever loses is IT. Deal?"

The girls shrug. Then Elle picks paper. Mariah picks scissors. Mariah wins; Elle is it.

And she's right back where she started.

Mariah walks away before we can even ask them to shake hands.

"I hope things get better," I say to Elle. I can't say, "I hope that helped," because I know it didn't.

"Everything always goes her way," Elle says.

Before she can walk back to her friends, I say, "Well, Elle, I'm glad I got to meet you and I know that wasn't the best

157

help ever, but I hope if you ever need to talk to someone, you'll find me, whether or not I'm wearing this shirt, okay?"

She smiles at me and nods.

I almost forget Gruber's there. Until he says, "Look! Cool! That kid just shoved the other kid's face into the water fountain! Come on, Naomi E. Let's go!"

CHAPTER TWENTY-ONE

Naomi Marie

"Memoir," says Katherine, looking like she wants us to pretend she just said "Cake!"

We don't.

"In fifth grade, many of you wrote personal narratives, but as you know, in middle school we are shifting to memoir. They both involve writing about your life. Does anyone know the difference?"

I do, because I did both in fifth grade, but I don't raise my hand. Ava called me an *overachiever eager beaver* yesterday, and while I kind of think it's good to achieve *more*, she didn't say it like it was a good thing. I don't think I want to be

Overachiever Girl at this school.

Katherine doesn't wait long for hands. "Personal narratives are just that—you tell a personal story, relay an event or small moment. But in memoir, I want you to think about both a memory and its meaning. There is reflection involved." When we just look at her, she smiles. "Why don't I just let you get to writing. As you've been working on your groups-and-memberships piece, you may have seen patterns in the topics that you chose, or come up with even more questions. Don't worry—a lot of what you're writing in your Writer's Notebooks now will help you with your memoir piece next month. Does anyone have any questions about what we've done so far?"

No one does, probably because no one really understands most of what we've done so far. At least I hope I'm not alone. We all take out our Writer's Notebooks and get started. Everyone except Jennifer, who's hiding a copy of *Teen Style* in her binder. As I pass her desk to go over and brainstorm with Gigi, I see that it's open to a picture of Mona Lisa, who's always wearing blond cornrows and booty shorts that say BABYCAKES on the butt, can't sing, and makes Momma start speechifying every time her name is mentioned.

"She is totally my spirit animal," whispers Jen to Ava. Or maybe it's Amanda. All Jen's friends' names seem to start with *A*; she's been trying to get people to say "J and the As," which is vomitociously annoying. I open my mouth without thinking.

"I don't think 'spirit animal' is a thing you should say," I whisper, rolling my eyes. "I heard on a podcast it's offensive." Which I kind of think Jen is, so maybe to her that's a compliment?

"Oh my God, are you calling me racist?" she loud-whispers, her eyes wide. "I can't believe you just said that."

Katherine looks up. "Naomi Marie, you can join Jennifer and Ava for quiet brainstorming or just sit down and get to work."

"Uh, I was actually going to work with Gigi," I stammer. I zip over to Gigi before Katherine can say anything else. We get straight to work, but I can feel Jen's eyes trying to burn a hole in my head. After a minute, I look up.

"Can I help you with something?" I whisper in my nicest mean voice. Her face is really red.

"That's so wrong, what you did," she whispers back. "What's wrong with saying 'spirit animal'? Hello, it's like right here in the magazine. And it's a Native American term, actually."

"First of all," I say, and I try to whisper even lower than her, "just because it's in a magazine doesn't make it right." I try to steady my voice. "And what do you mean by 'Native American term'? I don't remember the name of the podcast, but—"

"You just want to be offended about everything," Jen says. She turns to Gigi. "How do you deal? She's so annoying."

She glances at me. "And I trust *Teen Style* over you. Podcast, yeah right. You're just—"

"Just what?" I ask.

"Yeah," says Gigi, not whispering at all. "Just what?"

"Jennifer, Gigi, and Naomi Marie," Katherine calls out. "If you can't control yourselves, please let me know now. And if you're finished with your work, you can help others in the community. Are any of you finished?"

We all shake our heads. I glance over at Gigi, who looks like she's about to cry. I feel bad because she got called out for backing me up, but it felt good to have someone have my back like that. I turn and see Naomi E. staring at us with wide eyes.

"Sorry," I say to Katherine. I look down at my paper. Jen doesn't apologize; she just smirks and goes back to her magazine. She reads it for the rest of the period and never gets busted.

CHAPTER TWENTY-TWO

Naomi E.

Naomi Marie, Brianna, and I have our stuff spread out all over the kitchen table. The pineapple we had for after-school snack is long gone, but my left arm keeps landing in little puddles of its stickiness.

I've only crossed off one thing on my assignment pad. Math. And it was hardly anything—reviewing for a quiz. I have so much more to do.

I'm staring out the window at the small patch of colorless sky. I've been sitting like this for fifteen minutes, trying to think Creative Writing thoughts. Groups. Memberships.

I caught a quick glimpse of Naomi Marie's list of her

different communities, where she belongs. I don't know how many pages it was, but definitely more than one. And it's definitely due tomorrow, and I am still struggling to get the list under Groups I Belong To beyond these three: family, Drama Club, school/student. I mean, I'm friends with Annie, but that doesn't make us a community. And I guess I could count Peer Mediation, but that's just a class I have to take. I'm not sure what Katherine means.

Valerie walks in, and Brianna jumps out of her chair. "We are all doing homework TOGETHER!"

Valerie puts her stuff down and comes over to say hello. Then she reaches for the rag by the sink and runs it under the faucet. At the table, we lift our notebooks and pens and Brianna's crayons as Valerie mops up the sticky spots the pineapple left behind.

"Sorry, I meant to do that," Naomi Marie says.

Valerie nods in a way that means "don't worry about it." "What are you working on?" she asks, looking at Naomi Marie and me.

"Your kind of assignment, Momma," Naomi Marie says. "We listed our different groups and memberships, and now we're working on where they intersect, where they don't, that kind of thing."

Actually, I'm still working on the first part, but I don't announce that.

"I don't know what other homework E has, but once I

finish this, I'm done."

"Did you just call me E?" I ask.

Naomi Marie smiles. "Just trying it out. Never mind."

"Are you really almost done?" I ask. "And none of your teachers gave any homework?!"

"Oh, they did," she says. "I had extra time at the end of math. It wasn't a lot, so I just finished it then."

Already done!

I want to be done!

I was supposed to hang with Annie after school, but this is due tomorrow and I also have so much to read for science, a really long, not-a-lot-of-pictures chapter about lunar cycles and calendars and clocks, so I had to cancel. Annie sounded as disappointed as I am.

"Do you have a minute, Momma?" Naomi Marie asks. "I wanted to talk to you about what I heard about that Cranstock guy you and Ms. Starr were talking about. I heard some high school kids say—"

Brianna cuts her off. "And did I tell you that today we did art and we had to spread newspaper on top of the other newspaper but it didn't matter because when I spilled the gold glitter it knocked over the red glitter and a little of the blue and it went everywhere but I cleaned it all up, even though the colors got mixed, but rainbow glitter is the best glitter, right?"

"Hang on," Valerie says. "One at a time."

And even though this is how it is here—everyone does homework together at the kitchen table, and everyone talks the way I guess normal families do—I say, "If you don't mind, I think today I'm going to try writing in our room, M."

Naomi Marie looks confused, then laughs. "Yeah, okay. I get it. Like I said, I won't call you E again. You don't have to leave!"

I smile and say, "I think it might be easier for me to get my work done in our room." I gather up my stuff and go into the room I share with Naomi Marie.

Ugh, I've really let it get messy, and I know Naomi Marie hates that. I gather up the clothes that missed the hamper and stuff them in. And shoot, the three shirts with a book on top of them are all wrinkled now, so I add them to the hamper. I pick up my sneakers and rain boots and put them in the closet; and when I see Naomi Marie's shoes lined up neatly, I kneel down and try to make mine look better, but it's hard because we have more shoes than closet floor space.

I sit on my bed and pull the comfy red blanket onto my lap, under my notebook. My head starts to clear a little. Quiet is good. This was smart. How can you write when it's not quiet?

A quiet room is a good place to think about these things.

Where do I feel like I belong?

My mind tries to sneak back into our old house, where I lived with my parents and then with just my dad. And then into the backyard, in my garden. Oh. Garden. I'm a gardener, does that count? I write it down because it's better than nothing.

But no. This isn't about what we used to be. It's about what we are now. Where do I belong NOW? Where do I feel comfortable?

Ouch. That's a very hollow feeling, realizing there's no obvious answer.

Maybe that's the problem. Right now, I'm still figuring it all out. I belong to two families—and one of those is just Mom and me. Does that even count? I cross out Family and write down Family with Mom and Family with Dad, Valerie, Naomi Marie, and Brianna. That turns one answer into two.

Are we supposed to have pages of groups, like Naomi Marie?

There have to be others, but I can't think of them.

Ugh.

Turns out it's not that much fun thinking about how I don't really have places where I feel like I belong. I'd rather think about lunar cycles and finish up Creative Writing later (and that's really saying something). I get my science book from my backpack.

Valerie sticks her head in the doorway. "Is everything okay?"

I nod. "It's hard for me to focus sometimes when it's not

quiet," I say. In my whole life, the only time it wasn't quiet when I sat down to do homework was when I did it at Annie's house, and on those days I always ended up doing most of it once I got home.

"Okay," she says. "Whatever I can do to help you get your work done, I will always be happy to do."

I smile. "One thing that *always* helps me get my work done is a plate of cookies."

Valerie laughs. "Nice try."

CHAPTER TWENTY-THREE

Naomi Marie

Minute steaks for dinner, with sour cream mashed potatoes and roasted brussels sprouts. Dad made almost the same thing when Bri and I had dinner with him last week, which is kind of weird, but I'm not complaining. It's comforting, and I could use a little comfort food today. Naomi E. must have been really mad at me for calling her E; she didn't come out of our room until it was time to set the table. And I couldn't get a minute alone with Momma, so I'm waiting to bring up the Jen Incident. I'm trying to be patient; I don't fake-cough once while Brianna tells a long story about how even though she chose Water Table at Choice Time, Artie knocked the water table over, so she had to do blocks instead, which wasn't her choice, so it's not fair. Not Fair is, like, the little-sister slogan.

Tom gets up to take out the Ben & Jerry's so it will soften a little.

"What flavor?" asks Naomi E. I can see her fingers crossed under the table. I know she hates Cherry Garcia just as much as I do.

"Americone Dream," he says, and we all cheer.

Seems like the perfect opening.

"So the other day at school, somebody said 'spirit animal' and I'm pretty sure that's not cool, but . . ."

"Somebody meaning Jennifer Bile?" asks Naomi E. "*Such an appropriate last name.* Was that what you guys were arguing about in Creative Writing?"

I nod. "Yep. So I told her she shouldn't say that and she was kind of coming at me, saying that it was a Native American term and how I didn't know what I was talking about, and I know she's wrong, but . . . Katherine made us stop talking. I want to go back tomorrow and crush her."

"No need to talk about 'crushing' anyone," says Momma gently.

"It's Jennifer Bile, though," says Tom, and I give him a low five that Momma pretends she doesn't see.

"Momma, she said MONA LISA was her spirit animal," I say.

"That ridiculous appropriator, nonsinging wannabe—" starts Momma.

"Do what you want with meeeee, you got all I neeeeeeed," sings Brianna. "That's my favorite song!"

"That is NOT your favorite song," says Momma. "We do not sing Mona Lisa songs in this house."

"Hello! Back to spirit animal?" I say. "I remember they were talking about it on that podcast we listened to a couple of weeks ago, but I couldn't remember everything, and I didn't want to mess up. And you're a librarian . . ."

"Which means you're a superhero!" yells Brianna.

Momma grins. "Primary sources are my superpower!" she says, and I only groan a little. "But, honey, you're right, it's not cool. I hear it so much too; I see it on shirts, posters. . . . It was even a question in our staff team-building activities: 'Who is your spirit animal?' A group of us had to have a conversation with the facilitator about that. Usually, what people think they're referring to has specific sacred and cultural meaning to different Indigenous groups. That podcast—it was 'Soulquake,' by the way, if she wants to know—referenced the Ojibwe Nation. Oh! That reminds me—I just got a copy of a new young adult novel by an Ojibwe author—*Apple in the Middle* by Dawn Quigley. My school librarian book club is reading books for the next high school summer reading list. Can't wait to dig in!" Momma rubs her hands together like she's thinking about a giant slice of cake. "Anyway, there's not really any one 'Native American' anything, but people love to talk a lot of 'mystical universal Indian' nonsense."

171

"Yep, I've heard a lot of 'ancient Native American' sayings," says Tom. "And they're just not."

"Mmmhmm, like those vague 'African proverbs,'" says Momma, shaking her head. "Words and language matter. Would you use the term *gypped*? *Indian giver*? People say 'that's ghetto' to mean something negative. Think about 'off the rez.' What does that really mean?"

"Aaaand heere we go . . . ," I start. But I'm glad. This feels like home.

"Anyway," says Momma. "At best, she's misguided." Momma taps her fork. "If she wants to know more about the Ojibwe, tell your friend to read some Louise Erdrich, or to do some research on Winona LaDuke's work. Does she like sports? She can check out Grace White. You can too."

"I don't know if she really wants to know more about anything," I say. Naomi E. nods. "And she's not my friend. Plus she got mad at me for calling her out. Then *I* got in trouble for talking."

"Trouble?" says Momma, raising her eyebrows.

"I mean . . . Never mind, it's fine," I say. "I got this."

"But," starts Naomi E. When we look at her, she scoops up some potatoes. "Never mind." *But what?* I wonder.

"Ojibwe like Hungry Johnny?" asks Brianna. "I like to EAT EAT EAT! When are you going to read that to me again?"

That's one that I don't mind reading over and over. We both relate to Johnny having to respect the elders before he can get to his own food, like how it is at Christmas dinner.

We spend the rest of dinner playing Guess the Capital, and Bri surprises us all with Yaoundé and Budapest. She might be Geography Bowl material one day.

We use the caramel sauce that I made for last Saturday's waffles on top of our ice cream, and Naomi E. whips out a surprise box of cookies from Morningstar, which I've added to my list of great bakeries, and not just because they make amazing chocolate rugelach. She's my sister now; it's the right thing to do.

"How do you get all of your outfits planned out like that?" says Naomi E. as we pack up our backpacks for the morning. "I bet you already know what you're going to do for Wacky Hat/Hair Day."

"Actually, I was thinking about making a cake hat, but I don't know if that will be too weird. Ugh, what do you think Jen will do?" I ask. "Probably something over the top and rude."

Naomi E. is silent for a minute as she puts her colored pencils back into her Gudetama case. "Not that I'm making excuses for Vomitus Maximus, but *you* weren't even one hundred percent sure about spirit animal. How was *she* supposed to know? And she was kind of saying it in a good way, right?"

"Yeah, but when someone tells you something's offensive, I think you should at least consider that before you get all *de*fensive. You should have heard her."

"Ugh, no, I shouldn't have," says Naomi E. "But, um, I worry sometimes, you know," she says slowly. "About saying the wrong thing too. Not *Upchuck-iffer* wrong, but . . . we didn't talk about a lot of this stuff at my old school. Or in my old house. I don't want you to get mad at me."

"'Upchuck-iffer'—nice one," I say. She takes a little bow. "Actually, I kind of had that impression, you know, that you didn't talk about race very much before."

"I mean, those workshops and stuff, I never had to talk about being *white* before. It's kind of . . . weird. And uncomfortable. I like being comfortable."

"Yeah, I know you're pretty used to that," I say.

She frowns. "You sound like it's a bad thing. *I* didn't say that stuff; we're talking about Spewiffer."

"I know, I'm not saying that you did; it's just . . . I don't think you should worry as much about being told you're wrong like it's worse than actually *being* wrong."

We zip up our backpacks at the same time.

"I can't believe she likes Mona Lisa," says Naomi E. after a while. "It figures."

"Seriously!" I clear my throat. "But that remix of 'Snack You Up' is kinda hot."

"I'm glad you said it," says Naomi E. "Because, um . . . yeah. That's kind of my song."

We both smile, but we get ready for bed without talking anymore.

CHAPTER TWENTY-FOUR

Naomi E.

I lie in bed a long time thinking about what Naomi Marie said: *I don't think you should worry as much about being told you're wrong like it's worse than actually being wrong.* Those words sting in that way that I recognize (and wish I didn't). It happens when I hear something I wish wasn't true but that I kind of know is. It's something I actually *feel*, like a sore bruise that keeps getting poked.

I wish I could tell her how hard I'm trying to not let her down. I know we both have a lot of change to deal with, and I wonder if the changes she's had to make are easier or if it only looks that way because she always seems so sure of herself. Always.

That's sort of the perfect opposite of how I feel these days—sure of myself.

I don't know how late I fall asleep, but I know it's very late and that the only thing that gets me out of bed is knowing it's almost the weekend. When I'm tired like this, it feels like I'm only half there and not even a quarter-paying-attention.

But it would be impossible to miss this: in the hallway before third period, I notice Jen doing what looks like some nasty whispering to Ava, and I wonder if it's about Naomi Marie, who's getting something out of her nearby locker. I want to charge over and tell Jen and Ava to shut up, which is not exactly proper school behavior, but when I'm tired like this, I have about an eighth of the good judgment I usually have. I walk close and try to hear what she's saying, but they both look at me with big eyes that mean *What are YOU looking at?* And I don't hear anything. I can imagine, though. If I really did have a superpower, maybe I'd have had the courage to say something that covered everything at once—that Jen was so wrong and that I have Naomi Marie's back.

After school, Naomi Marie and Brianna go straight to their dad's, and when I get home, I find Dad outside, huffing and puffing. "I've been trying to haul this around back," he says, pointing at the not-even-close-to-as-good-as-a-garden planter where I grew a tomato plant this summer.

"I'll help," I say. "Let me put my backpack inside."

I do, and I look around the kitchen for something delicious but fail to find it. I take a banana instead and go sit on the front steps while I eat it.

"Moving it will be easy because of this," he says, showing me this little . . . I have no idea what it's called, but it has wheels. "If we can lift the planter onto it, we should be good to go."

I nod. Still eating. The plant's dead, and it wasn't that great when it was alive either. We got maybe five tomatoes. I've been trying to look forward to planting my garden for next summer, but it feels so far away—it's hard to even imagine. But then I remember: spring! And wait, even better, I don't have to wait! I never planted any spring-blooming plants in my old garden because I never thought I was a flower person. But I could start now. Spring bulbs get planted in the fall. And in the winter, when that first crocus shows through, it can be a happy reminder that the cold is almost over.

"Dad! Can we get bulbs, like to grow tulips and daffodils and crocuses?"

He shrugs and says, "I don't see why not. It would be a nice thing we can all do together—choose what plants, buy the bulbs, dig the holes. We'll have to get started soon, though. I think you have to do it in early fall maybe? Or just fall?"

My mouth's open, but words aren't coming out. Because

my garden has been my place for me to be alone. But now it's going to be for everyone. Another Yes, AND. I once would have been upset about this. Instead, I'm trying to be happy. We'll see.

"Ready?" Dad asks.

The planter is so heavy. And we are so uncoordinated. The one time we lift it high enough, the thing with wheels—Dad is calling it Dolly (I have no idea why he'd give it a name like that)—squirts away, and we end up putting the planter back down, for a second, on his foot. There's a reason Mom used to hire a handyman for around-the-house jobs that needed doing.

Luckily, he finds our inability to do even a simple thing as funny as I do, and we're laughing as we lift and miss Dolly again. "Should we wait until . . . umm . . . Valerie or Naomi Marie is here?" I ask. More hands, better coordination, maybe?

"We've got this," he says. And eventually, he's right. Once it's on Dolly, we roll her to the back of the house. Getting the big planter off Dolly is a lot easier than getting it on. Dad pulls out this plastic tarp thing, and we wrap the planter and shove it against the house.

"That looks ugly. I'll be hearing about it from Valerie," he says.

"Do you ever worry about saying the wrong thing to Valerie?" I ask.

He laughs and says, "Why would I worry about that? I have plenty of experience with saying the wrong thing with your mom." He looks at me. "Not funny?"

I shake my head. "I mean about her being black and us not . . ."

"Being black?" Dad asks, smiling.

I shrug. "It's hard for me to talk about."

"I get that," he says. "You're not used to talking about it, and that's on me. On me and your mom, really. But didn't we all start to work on that at the workshops we attended and . . . What?"

My hand is up, like a stop sign. "I want to talk to you about this, but I don't want you to assume I need more workshops. Can we talk without automatic workshop sign-ups?" He nods. "And can we go inside now?"

We do, and we sprawl out on the couches in the living room. I can't remember another afternoon when it's been just the two of us here, the way it used to be for so long.

"There's a lot I don't know, but I feel like there's always going to be. Things that just seem annoying or strange to me seem . . . different to Naomi Marie. Like remember I told you about when . . . umm . . . Valerie picked us up from Lisa Trotter's birthday party and Lisa Trotter's mother acted weird? I thought it was because we didn't show up at the party at the same time and also we have the same name! How was Lisa Trotter's mother supposed to know Valerie was picking me up, that Naomi Marie is my sister? She acted like it was definitely because she was black, and I really don't know if that was true."

"Hang on a sec," Dad says, and he goes into the kitchen. I hear him open the cabinet where Valerie's hiding the Halloween candy. He walks back in and drops a fun-size package of M&M's on my stomach.

"Thank you," I say.

"Maybe the way to start to do better is to ask questions," he says.

"Ask who?"

"Valerie? Maybe Naomi Marie."

"That would annoy Naomi Marie. Or make her mad. Or offended. She said something to me last night about how I'm too worried about being told I'm wrong, and that I should be worried about *being* wrong. My questions would just show her how wrong I am all the time, how little I know."

Dad goes back to the cabinet. I think we're going to need to buy a whole new bag of candy before Halloween. This time he drops a mini Twix on me. Mmm.

"Your questions will show you're trying. And as you get answers, you'll hear more stories and be more informed. Maybe you'll seek out more stories too, and become more aware of the privilege you and I have and the work we all need to do together for change."

It would be nice if there was just one part of my life that

wasn't about working at change.

Dad falls asleep. I go into Brianna's room. When Annie or I need cheering up, we sort of picture-read picture books to each other, ignoring the words and making up a story. Because picture books are the comfort food of reading.

But this is different. I'm here to read new-to-me books, to listen to stories Naomi Marie and Brianna grew up with. I plan to sort through and pick the ones that have black kids on the cover, but it turns out all the ones I reach for do.

I pull out *Seeds of Change, Ellington Was Not a Street, The Book Itch, Josephine: The Dazzling Life of Josephine Baker*. I grab another thick handful and take all the books into my room.

New-to-me stories.

It's a start.

CHAPTER TWENTY-FIVE

Naomi Marie

Carla puts two fingers in her mouth and whistles LOUD. The auditorium immediately gets quiet, which is pretty amazing, because ten seconds ago Aaron was yelling "DUDE!" over and over for no reason, Gruber was begging everyone in our Advisory to dare him to skateboard down the auditorium aisle, and Nina Bryant and her crew were doing the choreography for the "It's Over (And Over Again)" video.

Gigi whispers, "Thank you, Carla," and we give each other knowing looks because we both know it's a crime to do Adedayo like that. Especially when it's a duet with Airi; that song almost makes me cry every time I hear it because it's so beautiful. Me and Xio are going to make a video of us singing it next time we're at my dad's.

"Thanks, Chisholm," says Carla calmly as Assistant Principal Mark takes Gruber's skateboard away again. She introduces Amina and Ellison, who read the birthdays and announcements. Then Lulu from the Feminist Club comes up and flips her hair like it's on the US gymnastics team. She asks why no one is joining Feminist Club, even though the thing is that whenever anyone tries to ask her about joining, she says she's adding names to the wait list. Then we watch a short film made by the Old-School Video Games Club, which I might join.

Carla comes to take back the mic. "Oh, and the Wacky Hat/Hair Day parade will be here before you know it. Let's see how creative the Chisholm family can be!"

Cheers and whooping; Carla stands and looks at us until we're totally quiet again. It doesn't take long.

"I encourage each of you to remind your parents to actually read my weekly letters that offer MYRIAD suggestions on how all of us in our community can advocate for our rights, including for fully funded school libraries."

"Got that right!" yells Daisuke from the back. I know he's not the shushing kind of librarian, which I've never actually ever met in real life, but I didn't know he was the *yelling-from-the-back-of-the-auditorium* kind either! "Full-time school librarians are a right, not a privilege!" He gets lots of whoops, and I stand up and clap hard.

When I sit back down, Jennifer loud-whispers, "She is *such* a nerd, it's, like, ridiculous." I keep staring straight ahead, and Gigi squeezes my hand.

All of a sudden, a bunch of high schoolers stands up and starts chanting.

"No dirt with dirty money!" they chant over and over.

It's not that catchy.

Carla holds up her hand, but it doesn't work this time. More kids start chanting too, and I want to join in, even though I'm not sure if I should. Most of the teachers are shushing them, but a few are just sitting there.

"Is this about those flyers?" yells Gigi, trying to be heard over the crowd. "Why do they hate that Cranstock guy so much?"

"I think he has something to do with standardized tests or something," I say. "Momma—my mom doesn't really like him either."

I've been thinking that it was a good thing that some rich guy wants to give money to our school. But as I look around at the chaos in the auditorium, I wonder. I remember how Momma talked to Ms. Starr about "strings attached." I guess it's complicated. Like everything else.

Sun-dried tomatoes at the salad bar. Yuck. I'm glad I brought dessert from home, at least. Well, from Shelly Ann's.

"Not a fan?" says the boy who's serving as he watches me pick them out and put them on the side of my tray.

I shake my head. "They're just weird. They look like they're gonna be sweet like fruit leather, but they turn out to be salty and way more leathery."

"The only thing that should be leathery is a jacket like this, right?" He rubs the sleeve of his black-leather jacket. It looks older than Great-Uncle Lloyd.

"Mmmm," I say, which is a way of not saying what you think when what you think isn't very positive.

"I know, it looks ancient. Belonged to my grandpa. I'm a fan of all things vintage."

He's also wearing a fedora, a vest, and a tie. But with baggy jeans. "Uh, yeah, I guess."

"Anyway, just put them in the compost bin," he says. "Zero waste!" He hands me a flyer. It says there's going to be a meeting about the Chisholm funding "scam" in the playground across from school on Friday.

"Why is it a scam?" I ask.

"This guy is trying to do something good only to cover up worse stuff he's doing. The last school he 'helped' ended up having to switch all their tech and their textbooks to his company."

"We don't use textbooks here, though," I say.

"It's about control," says the boy. "Anyway, come to the meeting."

I go over to Gigi, who's waiting by the door with her bag lunch. We're going to have our lunch in the library and help Daisuke shelve books. "I would not have the nerve to talk to a tenth grader like that," she says. "Especially DeVante Swing."

"The salad bar guy? His name is DeVante Swing?"

"Well, really DeVante Johnson, but Swing is his nickname. He's the most popular boy in school. How do you not know that?"

I shrug. "Let's go upstairs. I don't want to spend the whole lunch period talking about someone named DeVante Swing."

"I'd be happy to use it talking *to* him, though, for real," says Gigi as we leave. I look back to where DeVante is using a salad spork as a mic as he sings "All Up in Your Face." He's not afraid to be silly, that's for sure.

"I guess he *is* sort of cute," I say.

Gigi holds up a hand for a high five, and I miss, which makes us completely crack up.

Katherine has been teaching us about our "writing territories," where you realize the things you care about by seeing what you write about over and over. I go through my Writer's Notebook and see Jenn Harlow and Jennifer Bile are all up in it. I can hear Xio say, *Why are you wasting time on them? You* know *they're not thinking about you!*

But *why* am I?

Asking myself why makes me think about the kids protesting the Eco-Casita and that Cranstock guy again. They don't really get in trouble; some of the teachers even seem to respect them even though they can get loud. And DeVante Swing—how does he make being silly look like the right thing to do? How can I do things like get good grades but act like I don't care about them? And learn how to dance without looking like I ever had to learn? How can I show up for justice and binge-watch *Idris Thompson, Teen Detective* all in the same week?

There were a couple of times today when I could have gone up to Jen, but I didn't. I don't know why. She thinks I don't see her chronic side eye. I don't want her thinking I'm scared of her. She's probably telling her stupid squad she shut me down. I need to be like Okoye from *Black Panther*. No respectable Dora Milaje would be worried about Jen Bile.

CHAPTER TWENTY - SIX

Naomi E.

Halloween is tricky when you're eleven. I still want to go trick-or-treating, but I feel too old for it. I'm a little jealous of Brianna, to tell the truth, because there's no question about it when you're in kindergarten. You are *all in* for Halloween. If I were Brianna, it would be simple—I'd be a trick-or-treating Makeda the Marvelous.

But today I am the luckiest person in the world because I am at Annie's! Which would be great on any day. But it's the most great today because they're putting up their Halloween decorations.

Every Halloween, they hang these giant ghosts in the

trees. Webs hang down from the roof. (Only Annie's dad is allowed on ladders, which seems like one of the strangest rules since he's the clumsiest person I've ever known. He once opened a cabinet and a mug fell out, shattered into pieces, one of which dug a big hole in his hand. He literally needed stitches just because he opened a cabinet.)

Annie and I are setting up the graveyard by their front steps when her little brother Chase comes out of nowhere to say, "Wanna know what Mom said no to this year?"

"Sure," I say. He's older than Brianna, and I used to find him so annoying, but today he's been fun to be around. He must have changed.

"No rotting corpses; no dead bodies in a bag or not in a bag; no dead dolls, especially if they're baby dolls; no heads with insides hanging out of the neck. But we have some new things—there's a Grim Reaper, and instead of putting all the ghosts in the tree, we're figuring out how to make them stand by the front door."

"Cool," I say.

"Naomi, can you grab that skeleton wreath?" Nice normal sentence, Annie. Skeleton wreath, sure. I reach for it, and it is exactly what she describes—the kind of wreath people put on their front doors, only made of bones.

It's so good to be with people who call me Naomi. Just Naomi. Not Naomi-e. My mom calls me Naomi too. It's a very small group of very excellent people.

"Oh, we bought this hook thing," Annie says. "I think it's—"

Her mom steps outside then, hook thing in hand. "Right here," she says. And then she looks at me, smiling and shaking her head. "We've missed you," she says.

Tears spring to my eyes because my body is great at mortifying me. "I've missed you all so much," I say. Annie doesn't have much free time because of soccer. And I have to divide my time between parents already. It doesn't leave a lot for hanging out. "I hope we can do this more often."

"We'd all like that," she says. "Why don't you two take a break inside now. I got you some goodies from that bakery you and your dad like so much, Morningstar."

That just about melts my insides into a buttery mess. "Thank you," I say.

Annie's looking at me like I'm an emotional alien. "Don't start crying. It's cookies. Just come on," she says, and I follow her inside.

There's a big box on the counter, and we open it to see what we're dealing with. Nice! I'm impressed by quantity— two of everything—and quality—she got the triple-chocolate chip cookies, and croissants, including two chocolate ones. Oh my.

"Milk?" Annie asks.

"Of course," I say.

She grabs it from the fridge, and I go to the cabinet and

admit I open it slowly in case some mug decides to take a tragic leap and break into pieces that make a hole in my hand.

We sit at the counter, and it's quiet at first because eating requires attention when the food you're eating is this kind of good.

"Mmm," I say.

"No lie," Annie says. Then she looks at me. "Tell me stuff. And next time I want to come to your house. I'm sick of my brothers. You're so lucky you landed in a family with sisters."

I smile, but I know it's not very convincing.

"What?" Annie says.

"Remember Beatrice Copley in fourth grade?"

"Duh. Yes. Wait, she's at your new school?"

"Ew, no, of course not." I pull the Morningstar box over. So much deliciousness to choose from. How about one of these M&M's cookies? Yes, thank you.

"I'm not saying Naomi Marie is like her in most ways, because she's not. But you know how Beatrice Copley was the girl every teacher picked for everything? And how she did extra credit even when it wasn't assigned? Well, Naomi Marie isn't like her, I mean, she doesn't act like she's better than me. But, wait. Let me ask—do you have a ton of homework this year? Like, way more than last?"

Annie shrugs. "There's more, but not a ton more. Do you want to split this coffee-cake thing?"

I nod. I want everything. "Chisholm's really hard. But

only for me, not for her. But it's not just school stuff. Like, remember when you asked, the first time you came over, if it was weird, the color thing? And I said it wasn't. Because it wasn't. But since then, I found out she thinks I don't care enough about race stuff, maybe?"

Annie is staring at me, mouth open, midchew.

"EW!" I say. "Close your mouth, disgusting-face!"

"Of course you care," she says, and I'm glad to hear it, even if it does mean seeing chewed-up coffee cake.

"I know. But I still say wrong things. And I don't know enough. And wait—you know how you're way smarter than your brothers?"

"Yeah," she says. Because it's just the truth.

"Well, she's a lot smarter than me. Or at least better at school stuff, and thinking about big things that I never thought about. And it's . . . I don't know if I'm going to be in trouble with my dad and Valerie, because there's no way I'm going to do anywhere close to how she does in school."

Annie nods like she's getting it. "And when you were an only child, you were always the smartest one and the best student. The best at everything."

I feel like there's a lot more to say. But in a way, Annie just summed it all up. So we sit and eat, and it is so, so good.

CHAPTER TWENTY — SEVEN

Naomi Marie

"Oxtail!" Brianna yells as she runs past Daddy into the kitchen. I hug him and walk at a more dignified middle school pace, even though I'm really hungry and I can smell all kinds of goodness.

"Yep," says Daddy proudly. "And stew peas . . . jasmine rice . . . of course some callaloo."

"Yay everything except callaloo!" says Brianna. "Daddy, I made a baguette in school." She takes out a piece of what used to be bread. "I saved you a piece. Question: Do you have butter?" She opens the fridge.

"Brianna, that's too old and stale for Daddy to eat," I say.

"You'll poison him."

Brianna's lip gets all poked out for a second; then she looks up. "Like a fairy tale? Oooh, then what would he turn into?"

"A big bunch of callaloo," says Daddy, trying to pick us both up. It doesn't work. "Oof, you girls are getting big." He turns to me and mouths, *Thank you.*

"I'm thinking I should call you Pops," I say. "My favorite character on *Ocean Hill* calls her parents Guidance and Pops; she's in sixth grade too. Can we watch *Ocean Hill* tonight, Daddy? After Brianna goes to bed?"

"No watching shows without me," says Brianna calmly. "Momma says." I stick my tongue out at her.

"Guidance?" asks Daddy. He shakes his head. "Never mind, I'm sure I don't want to know. And we are not going to be watching shows tonight. After we enjoy this sumptuous feast—"

"S-U-M-P-T-U-O-U-S, sumptuous," I say automatically. "Easy peasy."

"As I was saying, you both clearly have a lot to tell me, and I have much to share with you, and I worked like a dog to take a cab all the way to Islands to get this food, so we are going to finish it all and talk the night away!"

"Games?" I ask.

"You know it," says Daddy. "Including Bananagrams."

Yes!

"Sounds good to me," I say. "Let's eat. I'm so hungry I

could eat all of this!"

"You have to do portions," says Bri. "I know about MyPlate, Daddy. First Lady Forever Michelle Obama said that it's all about portions. I learned that in school."

"And I'm so proud of you," says Daddy. "Let's celebrate with DINNER!"

One of the great things about being at Daddy's is that since we're already eating on the fluffy L-shaped couch, we only have to shift a little and roll away from our empty plates when we're done.

"Whoa," says Brianna, patting her stomach. "My belly has a lot of portions inside."

I pour us all some sorrel. "Pops, I need some advice."

"Pops? What happened to Daddy? I am going to be your daddy forever, and—"

"—Just like First Lady Forever Michelle Obama!"

"Exactly." Daddy nods as he scoops us both up into a hug. "Just like First Lady Forever Michelle Obama. Even if you are in *kid*-nergarden and middle school. You'll always be my little girls."

"See?" Brianna says to me. "Daddy says it the special way too."

"I can't keep calling you the same thing she calls you, Dad," I say, glaring at Bri.

"White Naomi doesn't call Momma anything," Bri says.

I think about that for a second. I didn't realize it, but I guess she doesn't. Should I ask her why? She'll probably tell me to let it go, like everything else.

"*Anyway,*" I say. "Daddy, remember I told you that this rich guy is giving money to our school?"

"Eco-Casiiiiitaaaaaa," sings Bri.

"Uh-huh," Daddy says. "I really like the things they're doing there. Your mother worked hard to get you all spots in that school."

"Eco-Casiiiiiiitaaaaaaa," sings Bri.

"Well, I went to a protest meeting. . . . A lot of people are against it."

"Follow the money," says Daddy. When I just look at him, he adds, "Sorry, *All the President's Men* reference. Classic film. We'll watch it next time."

"But my teacher says we'll get new equipment," says Bri. "It's gonna teach us a lot of science, and I am going to be a scientist. And a tightrope waaaaaalker."

"Yeah, so anyway," I say, "me and Gigi—"

"Gigi's your BFF?"

"Don't say 'BFF,' Daddy—it's embarrassing . . . and yeah, she's my good friend at school. But she's not replacing Xio or anything. Me and Gigi wonder if it's okay for him to help the school even if he's not so great."

Daddy nods slowly. "Well, I can see that it's complicated. Have the protesters talked to the administration?"

"Question: What's ministration?" asks Bri. I'm glad she stopped with the singing. "Eco-Casiiiiiitaaaaaaa!"

I thought too soon.

Then she jumps up and adds a little dance. I have to laugh.

Daddy turns to me.

"It's, like, who's in charge; at school it's Carla," I say to Bri. "Also, it's spelled *A-D-M-I-N-I-S-T-R-A-T-I-O-N*."

Daddy nods. "On one hand, you don't necessarily want to be in bed with an organization or individual that doesn't reflect the values you stand for . . . but it's also true that people can do good work *and* do things we disagree with."

"Question," starts Brianna.

"He means sometimes people are good and bad at the same time; we can't always judge," I say quickly. "Or they *do* bad and good things."

"On *Community Court*, there's always a judge," Bri replies.

"Different kind of judge," I say. I'm quiet for a minute. "I think I need more information before I can make up my mind about this whole thing."

"Whatever you do or don't find out, you have to decide for yourself what you stand for. Sometimes that takes a while. And that's okay. Rushing to judgment is never a good thing."

"Amber drew a line on the edge of the sand table," says Bri. "In marker. That's not appropriate. I told on her."

"Don't be a snitch," I say.

"On *Community Court*, the judge always pounds her

hammer on the high table," says Brianna, ignoring me. "Question: Is Carla going to have a hammer? What if she pounds you by mistake?"

"Oooh, *Community Court!*" says Daddy. "I love that show!"

"I don't think you're supposed to encourage her," I say.

"And speaking of not watching inappropriate TV," Daddy says quickly, "who's up for Bananagrams?"

"ME!" I yell right along with Bri.

"Okay, I'll set us up. Teams?"

"You get Bri," I say, fast. She's always trying to make me use "words" like *ackinopolis* in word games.

Daddy laughs and high-fives Bri. "We will be unstoppable!" he says. "Naomi Marie, why don't you check the kitchen counter. I believe there are some coconut cupcakes from Shelly Ann's in there."

"Woot!" As I head to the kitchen, I turn back. "Oh, wait, Daddy, didn't you have something to tell us too?"

"Oh! Yes, I do." He pauses, and I hold my breath, just in case it's something bad that I have to pretend is good. Like . . . a serious girlfriend, or *ladyfriend*, as Xio says. I'm still getting used to Tom. I need Daddy to be just Daddy for a little longer. I realize suddenly that I don't want to call him Pops.

"I'm going to get . . . a dog!" says Daddy. "And I want you girls to come to the shelter with me tomorrow so we can meet the newest family member together."

"YAY!" shouts Bri, dancing around again. And maybe I do too. *A dog!* This is way better than a ladyfriend! "When you read *Weekends with Max and His Dad* to me, Naomi Marie, we can talk about doggy names!"

"I thought you asked Naomi E. to read that to you already," I say, trying to sound casual. "When did I say I'd read it?"

"I've been saving it for you because we have weekends with our dad. And you don't have to say you'll read to me. It's like you don't have to say you love me every day. I know you will, forever. Just like—"

"First Lady Forever Michelle Obama," I say, scooping my little sister into a hug.

"Also, remember when we used to play *Ranger in Time*? And you put my water dish—"

"Yay, Daddy's getting a dog!" I say quickly, hugging her again. "Daddy, can I text Xio before we start? I have to tell her about this!"

"She's on her way over," says Daddy, smiling. "That's my other surprise." I hug him, and Bri does too, because she keeps forgetting that Xio is *my* friend.

"You are the best at surprises," I say. "Like, you totally win at them!"

As the doorbell rings, I think about how I was just happy to be sleeping over at Daddy's tonight and I got bonus dog news *and* Xio. Maybe Josh Cranstock is becoming a good guy, or at least better. Maybe DeVante Swing will think that I'm the most mature sixth grader he's ever met. Maybe Jen Bile will stop being racist without me saying anything, and Naomi E. will start saying something about *anything*.

I think back to Emma's smug smile and Waverly's frowning face. Lisa Trotter's mom and Jen's . . . everything.

Maybe.

CHAPTER TWENTY - EIGHT

Naomi E.

I packed myself the best lunch—peanut butter and banana (and I snuck in Marshmallow Fluff when Valerie wasn't looking). And a bag of pretzels, which Edie is eyeing. "Are those sharing pretzels?" she asks.

I nod. "There's another Drama Club meeting after school today. Please come!"

Edie wrinkles up her nose. "I can't. Orthodontist."

"Oh my goodness," I say. "What IS that?" Edie unwraps a sandwich that is so big—so tall!—there's no way she can fit it into her mouth. But she does, kind of, and takes a huge bite.

"Eeseanmato," she answers.

Her sandwich is only a tiny bit shorter than her face. I start laughing and so does she, but it's hard, with a mouth full of eeseanmato (whatever that is). She puts up her index finger in a let-me-chew way.

"I'm sorry," I say, still laughing. "*What* is it?"

Before she can answer, Gruber is standing next to me in his bright-yellow Peer Mediation shirt. "You gotta do peer mediation," he says.

I shake my head. "I checked the website. It is not my turn, and I'm not the alternate."

"Sawyer was supposed to be my partner today but he's absent."

"Like I said, I'm not the alternate." I always check the calendar and pack my shirt when I'm the alternate, just in case.

"Yeah, I know," he says. "Lauren's the alternate, but she went home with pink eye."

"Ew," Edie says. Her sandwich has fallen apart. (I'm thinking it's cheese and tomato.)

My eyes start itching, thinking about pink eye.

"I was patrolling by myself, but Harris saw and said I need a partner, and when I told him they were absent he said to get you."

Universe, you have got to be kidding. I was only supposed to be teamed with Gruber once. One time. This is the third.

I grab my stuff and say good-bye to Edie.

"There are two kids who need a mediation, but it's with

girls and I just can't deal," he says.

Gruber, I don't even have words.

I thought we were going outside, but he brings me to a corner of the cafeteria. Two girls sit across from each other not looking at each other.

"Do you want to try mediation?" I ask. Maybe they'll say no and I can go back to Edie.

One girl's arms are folded over her chest, hands below her shoulders, like she's hugging herself. For courage, maybe. It seems like she can't look up at the other girl. Looking directly at the table, she says, "Every day, Birdie says my lunch is weird or that it smells or who could even eat that. She says it really loud so everyone hears. And I wish she could mind her own business because . . ." She stops talking.

Gruber's looking around, then loudly asks some random kid, "Are you gonna eat that?" pointing at a doughnut. My partner, ladies and gentlemen!

"Okay," I say, since I'm going to have to do this myself. "Before we started, I should have said you'll each have a turn to talk, no interrupting, no name-calling; we'll try to come up with a compromise together." I really hope we can do better than rock/paper/scissors.

Birdie sits up straight and looks at the other girl. "I don't say it every *day*, Prisha, but your lunch does smell, and she keeps sitting right behind me, so it's not like I can just not smell it. And once I smell it, I'm sorry, but I lose my appetite."

I have learned that *I'm sorry, but* is not the most sincere kind of apology.

"Do you both feel like you've shared your side of the story?"

Birdie shrugs one shoulder. Prisha doesn't respond.

I repeat back to them: "Prisha feels hurt that Birdie talks about how her lunch smells. Birdie . . ." I can't think of how to say it without making Birdie sound awful. (Because Birdie is awful.)

"And Birdie," Gruber says, "was nasty."

"NO NAME-CALLING, GRUBER! And Birdie doesn't think she did anything wrong."

"Prisha?" I ask. "Is there anything else you want to say? Like how that makes you feel?"

"Sad," Prisha says. "She's not nice to me. I can't name everything. But the lunch, that's where she's meanest in front of the most people."

Birdie does not wait to be asked. She says, "We're not friends. I can't be everyone's friend. But I'm *not* mean." She turns to Gruber. "And you said that we just had to talk about what happened when you said we should do medation, or whatever you call it."

"Mediation," I say automatically.

No matter what we do here, Birdie's not suddenly going to be kind to Prisha. It makes me feel a little hopeless. Like peer mediation might be a waste of time.

"Do either of you have any ideas for how to resolve this conflict?" I ask.

Neither one says anything.

Finally, Prisha says quietly, "Well, I'd like her to apologi—"

"I'm not saying I'm sorry for saying your food smells. Your food does smell! Ask anyone!"

"Hang on," I say. "Do either of you have any other ideas about how to avoid this in the future? Birdie?"

"She could sit someplace else so I don't have to smell it."

I'm supposed to have a nonjudg-y face, but Birdie is not making this easy. "Someone could change her table, sure. Or maybe you could try to keep comments that aren't nice to yourself," I say. I'm not sure this is exactly how Harris would want me handling this, but I'm just being realistic.

"And I'd like her to not be mean to me," Prisha says. She's looking directly at Birdie now. "Stop being mean to me," she says. Well, that's something. She's speaking up for herself. Which is hard.

"What do you think, Birdie?"

Birdie shrugs again (it makes me want to never shrug) and says, "Yeah, I'll be nice." It is perfectly clear: she doesn't mean it.

"Can you shake hands?" I ask. It's the symbol of a successful mediation. Not that this feels all that successful.

They do, and then Birdie asks, "Can I go now?"

I nod. "You can go too, Prisha."

Gruber and I head outside to patrol the schoolyard, but before we're halfway to the fence, this little girl comes over and says, "Excuse me? Are you the ones who help when there's a problem?"

I smile at her because that's the kind of superhero description I was thinking of when I signed up for this. "What's happening?"

She has good instincts—she ignores Gruber completely—and takes my hand to lead me somewhere. "This girl is accusing me of doing something bad and . . ." Her voice is sad sounding, and she stops walking. In a quiet voice she says, "I did do it, that's the hard part; but it was an accident, and I feel so bad."

I'm not supposed to let her start telling her story until we have both people involved together. But it's hard not to feel bad for her—she looks so upset. And though I'm supposed to be completely impartial, I find I'm almost always drawn to the side of the person who seeks out the peer mediators. They're usually the ones who need us more.

"What's your name?" I ask.

"Emma," she says. "What's yours?"

"Naomi E.," I say.

Emma points at a girl who looks like she's trying not to cry. "She's the one who's saying I did it on purpose," she says.

The girl is standing on a big patch of multicolored chalk mess.

"I'm Naomi E.," I say. "A peer mediator. Can you tell me what's going on?"

"I was making a chalk mural—do you know the book *Tar Beach*? I was making a chalk mural of Cassie flying, only instead of over Harlem, she's flying over Chisholm."

"That's amazing," I say. "I just read that book for the first time! My little sister has it. A mural is such a great idea."

"Yeah," Emma says. "It is a great idea."

"If it was a great idea, why did you ruin it, Emma?!" Waverly is screaming. "I worked on it for so long. It took up this whole space," she says, using her arms to show the patch between the swings and the school. "And she walked right over it, back and forth, like shuffling her feet so she really ruined it!"

"Whoa," I say. "Slow down. There are rules for peer mediation. No screaming is one of the big ones. No name-calling. Together we'll try to come up with a fair solution."

Waverly won't meet my eye. I wish I got to the rules before she started screaming—I feel bad shutting her down like this.

Emma's mouth is wide open. "Waverly! Why don't you believe me? It was an accident! And you don't have to yell. I feel really bad!"

I look around for Gruber, but I seem to have lost him. Naomi Marie is leaning against the fence; is she watching us? Kids start lining up at the door—the bell's going to ring any minute.

Before Waverly can answer, I say, "Let's go sit down and talk about it."

"This is one of those meteorations, Waverly," Emma says. "Naomi E. is going to help us solve our problem." She reaches up and takes my hand.

"It's mediation, Emma!" Waverly yells. "You can't even pronounce it!"

"Actually, we don't have time for a whole mediation right now, but quickly—Waverly, Emma says it was an accident, that she didn't mean to ruin your mural. Do you want to accept her apology?"

The bell rings. Waverly looks at me. "She *didn't* apologize!" She looks right at Emma and yells, "I know you ruined my mural on purpose."

I want to help. I should be able to help. "We can talk about this some more tomorrow," I say. "We could meet at the start . . ." Waverly turns and storms back into the school. Emma smiles and follows Waverly into the building.

CHAPTER TWENTY-NINE

Naomi Marie

Today is one of those fun days in Creative Writing when we get to spend half of the double period talking about all the different books we're reading. It's like an in-school book club! We ask each other questions like "Who has the power in this story?" and pay attention to the number of white-girl book cover models and the number of silhouettes who are supposed to represent people of color. Since some of the Reading Buddies are in this class, and we'd still be talking book talk, I ask Katherine if we can go to the library to do some planning for our next session. Even though I'm supposed to pay attention to both Waverly's and Emma's needs, I want to find something especially for Waverly today. When I saw Waverly walk away from that "mediation" all alone and Emma smile at Naomi E. like she'd won AGAIN . . . I *knew* what went down. I want Waverly to know that I see her, all of her.

"I can't talk about books without food," says Gruber as we leave the classroom. "We need doughnut holes."

"Why are you here again?" asks Gigi.

Seriously, I think. He's not even a Reading Buddy; I've heard some stories about him from Naomi E. But I know: he annoys everyone, so Katherine wants us to set examples, be leaders, blah blah blah. I guess what she doesn't want is for us to get anything done. But we're trying. And I'm trying to find that *one nice thing* about Gruber that I can focus on.

"So," I say, after we settle at a round table, "I need suggestions for something that's about social justice." I point to Gigi. "We read *The Alphabet Tree* with our kids, and they got really into it." Gigi and AnnMarie give me snaps, but Gruber just looks at me.

"Isn't your mom a librarian?" he asks. "Just ask her."

"I'm *going* to ask her, and Daisuke too, but the first rule of school librarianship is utilizing all available resources—including people. Most of you guys are Reading Buddies, so . . ."

"You're not a school librarian, though," he says. "So those are not your rules."

Sigh. I just don't answer.

"When you say social justice, what do you mean?" asks Daisuke, who is pretending to shelve books nearby. That's how he monitors our conversations. He thinks we can't tell, so we just let him believe that. "Can you elaborate, Naomi Marie?"

"Well . . . ," I say. "I really want something about kids doing stuff, being leaders and activists. But also good stories. Like in this book *Piecing Me Together*, the main character is smart and creative and has all these ideas, but because of where she's from and because she's Black, even the people who are supposed to be helping her kind of don't listen to her at first. But she ends up being a leader and feeling stronger because of who she is, no matter what other people see or think."

"I want to read that," says AnnMarie. "I wonder if Daisuke—"

"Yes," says Daisuke, and he drops the book on the table in front of her. We all laugh.

"Can I get it next?" asks Gruber. I raise my eyebrows but don't say anything.

"What about writing?" asks Gigi. "We have Suggestion Boxes in Community Builders but nobody's really using them. Maybe after we read to the kids, they can do a really short Baby Reader Response."

"Just don't call it 'baby,'" says AnnMarie.

"I have a fruit leather," whispers Gigi. "Who wants some?" A couple of kids hold out their hands and she starts tearing off little pieces. It feels very *subversive* and I like it, even though I feel kind of bad too. Is that how revolutionaries feel?

"Here you go," says Daisuke, appearing next to me with a stack of books in his hands. "Just remember, guys, you have special eating privileges because I trust you. No crumbs, no trash."

We each only get a tiny bit of fruit leather, but it's kind of a mood boost, and we start talking and looking on the shelves for books. We find some good ones—*Last Stop on Market Street, Rad Women Worldwide, Separate Is Never Equal*; and Daisuke gives us *Hands around the Library, This Is the Rope*, and *The Amazing Age of John Roy Lynch*. Gruber recommends a book about Ida B. Wells (Gruber!!! Reads!!! Ida B.!!!). I wonder if he's trying to change his image too, but then he burps so loud, Daisuke makes him leave the library.

At recess, I see Naomi E. and Edie standing by the swings, and I run over to them.

"E, can I talk to you for a sec?" I ask.

She frowns and nods, and we move over the slide. "Uh, please stop trying to make 'E' happen!"

"Sorry, sorry . . . anyway, I wanted to tell you—about Gruber—"

"Voldemort's little brother? A goblin who will show his true self on Halloween? Everything annoying about boys all rolled into one? Yes, I know." She laughs a little.

"I know he can be a pain, but he was just talking about books, and he was almost . . . okay, for a minute. Maybe if you just kind of act nice to him—"

"Seriously?! You're serious right now. The same Gruber who makes gagging sounds whenever Katherine says the word *period*. The Gruber who would literally start a fight just so he would have something to mediate?" She rolls her eyes. "Give me a break."

"Okay, that period thing is inexcusable, but—"

She puts up a hand. "I've had to spend way more time with him than you, so just stop."

"Speaking of that, I saw you with Waverly and Emma yesterday, and I think—"

"Okay, you're not even a mediator yet, and you're telling me how to do that too? I know you're the family leader, but I've been working hard at this, and I can handle it." She stomps off, and I stand there, not even sure what just happened.

"What just happened?" asks Gigi when I slide to the ground along the fence next to her. "Your sister looked kind of mad."

"I have no idea," I say. I guess she really doesn't like me calling her E.

***

A few minutes later, Jen and her minions walk by, and Jen makes a big point of staring at me, then rolling her eyes and looking away. They stand in a big clump nearby and keep whispering and looking over. Then they come right up to me. She looks me up and down, turns to her friends to laugh, and then walks away slowly.

"Gross," says Gigi.

"My sentiments exactly," says Gruber, coming over. I don't know what's more surprising, the fact that Gruber said something like "my sentiments exactly" or the fact that he has those sentiments at all. Suddenly, Jen, smiling, waves me over. Huh?

"Me?" I say. And she nods, still smiling. I walk over carefully. "What's up?"

She takes out a bag. "So, I'm going to wear this for Wacky Hat/Hair Day and I wanted to let you know in advance so you don't call me racist again." She takes out one of those stupid rainbow Afro wigs that some people (annoying people) use for clown costumes. "It's kind of like your hair, right?" I was so proud of my Afro puff this morning.

I can't speak.

"Yo, what is that thing?" asks Gruber. "Is it alive?"

"Ask Naomi Marie," says Jen, smiling and putting it on. Her minions giggle.

"You're not funny," I say. "I don't have . . . clown hair."

"Lighten up," says Jen. "It's a joke. And you still haven't apologized for calling me a racist. That's bullying, and my parents are going to be getting in touch with Carla about it. And if the wig fits . . ."

"*I'm* not a costume," I say. "And *bullying*? You are so ignorant."

"Ha, for your information, I took the test for Garfield, so I'll be in a gifted and talented school next year, away from all of you—"

"All of you what?" asks Gigi.

"Yeah, what?" asks Gruber.

"Whatever," says Jen. She takes an Afro pick out of her back pocket; it has a fist for a handle, just like one that we have at home. She sticks it in the wig and walks away, laughing with her friends.

I feel embarrassed and furious and ashamed and all sorts of things. I can't really speak. Gruber very awkwardly punches my arm and mutters, "She's an idiot," and wanders away. Gigi, kind of the way a best friend would, talks about Adedayo and Airi and books and board games. I can tell she's doing it to show that we're having fun. So I try to, even though I'm angry at Jen, worried about Naomi E., surprised by Gruber, and confused about . . . almost everything else. I don't even think a list could clear things up right now.

CHAPTER THIRTY

Naomi E.

Katherine handed back what was supposed to be my final draft of the Communities/Where I Belong essay. Like she did on my early drafts, Katherine asked to talk to me after class, then told me that I need to write more, try harder, spend more time, dig deeper, explore new ways of thinking. She said if my assignments don't get better soon, it might be time to come in for extra help on Thursday mornings, when she can work with me; but I can't imagine a way to explain that to Naomi Marie or my parents without them knowing things I'd rather they didn't know.

I got as much of my homework done before dinner as I

could, and now I'm back at the kitchen table. If I work in bed, like I do some days, I'll just fall asleep. The kitchen is quiet at night when everyone's off doing other stuff— Brianna's in the bath. I don't know what Naomi Marie is doing, but it's definitely not homework, because she finished it long ago. I still haven't finished six math problems, and I keep putting off Creative Writing because it's awful and there's this whole other Katherine assignment too and suddenly Dad and Valerie are sitting with me.

"Still doing homework?" Dad asks.

What else would I be doing at the table with my textbooks all around me? I take a quick look to make sure the marked-up Creative Writing assignment isn't showing. My math text is covering it completely.

I nod.

"Almost done?" Valerie asks.

I shrug, but they don't leave. They sit there looking at me, so I say, "Not really."

"Is there anything we can do to help you get your assignments done?" Valerie asks. "Did working in your room help? Because you are free to do that. And tell her about the workshop—"

Brianna's voice cuts through everything: "Momma! Is there new shampoo? This one's empty and I have soap in my eyes and—"

"I'll be right there," Valerie calls back, a look of apology on her face. I just smile, because the sooner we stop talking, the sooner I can get back to trying to finish. But first I'm pretty sure I have to hear about a workshop.

Dad says, "So I went to this workshop through Valerie's school, for helping kids with organization. And study skills. That kind of thing."

"You did?"

He nods, excited. "Do you want to show me all the homework you have, and maybe we can put our minds together to see if there's a more efficient way to do it? Do you have each assignment written down?"

"Dad! Of course I have them all written down!" I point at the assignment pad. "A page and a half. I just have a lot of homework. I need to—"

Naomi Marie steps into the kitchen and says, "Naomi E., have you seen my library card? I know I left it on the dresser, but your stuff was piled up there and now it's not, so maybe when you put away your laundry or something— Did you see it?"

"Want me to help you look?"

Dad says, "Keep looking, Naomi Marie. Naomi E. has some work to finish."

And here's the thing. I know they're both thinking, *Even though Naomi Marie also had a lot of work but finished it a really long time ago. And Naomi E.'s parent had to go to a workshop for kids who can't do all their work.*

"Dad?" I say. "Can I please get back to this?"

He nods. "Let me just show you a couple of things. I got you these highlighters and Post-it notes so you can organize your assignments, maybe according to how long you think they'll take so you can structure your time better. Also, I was thinking maybe I should ask for a meeting with your teachers because it seems like maybe you're struggling a little and—"

"What? Dad! No! My homework's taking me too long, I know, so I'll do better, get it done faster, but no! I'll use the color stuff, but do not call my school. Really. Promise me you won't."

He nods, which I'm pretty sure is the same as a promise. And I get back to work.

An hour and a half later, Brianna's been asleep for a while and Naomi Marie is in bed. I am still at the table. Actually, part of me is *on* the table—my arm is out flat across it and my cheek leans against my upper arm. It's not comfortable, and the table smells like super-lemon from the cleaner we use, and if I fall asleep I'll wake early and can finish my work then. But also I know that makes no sense, and without warning I feel tears pooling, because even though I finished my math, I still have to try to make my memberships thing longer and write my response to the book Katherine read as an "intro to the complex and inspiring world of memoir." It was called *Dancing to Freedom* and it was pretty good, but she wants us to brainstorm ideas for our own memoirs and to show how that book inspired us.

I don't get how we're supposed to make those big kinds of connections. The kid in the book was living a horrible life in China—not enough food, not enough money—and had a chance to train as a dancer and he worked hard, blah blah, blah, and made his dreams come true.

I know I don't face the challenges the author did. So I get the comparison there. But the dreams-come-true part? I can't even figure out where my memberships are—I'm supposed to have all my dreams worked out too?

I close my eyes for a minute, to maybe think about what I can write that won't make Katherine need to talk to me after class. Or maybe I can rest, for a minute, just a quick minute. Close my eyes for one minute. Or less than a minute. It'll be okay.

I feel someone squeeze my hand. "Honey, go to bed," Valerie says. "You can get up early to finish this."

She has to be thinking about how long ago Naomi Marie finished. How Naomi Marie doesn't sleep on her arm at the table while doing her homework. How only one sixth-grade student here needs color-coded highlighters and Post-it notes. But all I can do is nod and shuffle to bed.

CHAPTER THIRTY - ONE

Naomi Marie

In the morning, I realize that Naomi E. got about as much sleep as I did, which is none. I want to tell her about Jen and her stupid wig, but she never explained why she had such an attitude yesterday, and anyway, I'm tired of Naomi E. telling me to just ignore Jen.

We don't talk much as we get ready for school, but I pass her the Trader Joe O's and almond milk, and she brings my backpack to the door so that I can pick it up on our way out.

"You girls are quiet this morning," says Momma. It's kind of stating the obvious and not a question, so I don't say anything. Neither does Naomi E., and I know she's thinking the same as me.

"Maybe they were playing apps," says Bri. "They're SCREENAGERS, you know. There's a movie. They're going to show it at school on Friday night and I want to go."

"It's for middle schoolers, babyhead," I say. "And you don't even know what you're talking about."

"Remember, um . . . your—Val—your mom takes our phones every night," says Naomi E. She doesn't sound stank anymore. I want to ask what the problem was, but more than that, I want her to just tell me.

"And they definitely don't have apps, Bri," I say. I pause for a second. "Naomi E., what exactly do you call my mom?"

"Wait, what? Um . . . what do you call my dad?"

"Tom!" Bri and I both say.

"Everybody knows that," adds Bri, rolling her eyes.

Naomi E. kind of laughs. "Oh yeah, right." She shrugs. "I'm still working on that."

"It's taking long enough," I say.

"Well, as we learned in the Go Forth, Family workshop, sometimes these things take time, and we're allowed to take all the time and space we need."

"Oh, I guess you *were* listening," I mutter. "I wasn't sure because you never talked."

"There wasn't much for me to say, actually," she says. "And you seemed to care so much about everything, I figured *you* needed the time and space to talk more."

"Are you serious right now?" I ask.

"Ooooh, that's her grown-up Serious voice," says Bri. "She even said 'serious' in it."

"What?" asks Naomi E.

"So are you saying you didn't care? That you *don't* care?" I ask. "Seriously?! I knew it."

"Wait, no . . . what are you talking about?"

"You always act like I just have . . . issues or something. Like my Blackness is . . . a problem for me to get over, or an inconvenience for you."

"I don't understand what's going on," says Naomi E.

I think back to Waverly looking so defeated by Emma and her slickness. Like she knew she'd never win. "I bet you just assumed Emma was telling the truth because she's white and acted all sad. You were holding hands with her and talking all soft, leaning in to listen to her. You have no idea how shady that girl is. And then you had that attitude for no reason. . . . I just don't even know what to say right now."

"I'm really not understanding. . . . First of all, you were ridiculous about Gruber," she says. "I'm the one who's been working with him all this time. And with Emma and Waverly, I was being a mediator, trying to listen to both sides. Waverly was the one yelling and screaming in Emma's face—I didn't have to lean in to hear her. I don't think—"

"No, you really don't sometimes," I say softly, "And it

hurts. This time it really hurts." Now it's all pouring out of me. "You know, you're supposed to be my sister. Whenever I want to talk to you about how ridiculous and RACIST Jen is—" I stop.

"'Supposed to be'?" Naomi E. whispers.

"Don't cry, okay?" says Bri softly. "Oh wait—it's okay to cry, I forgot."

Since both Naomi E. and I are crying, I'm not sure who she's talking to.

"Girls, you are going to be late!" calls Momma from the living room. "And that will make me late, and that is not a good thing."

"I just didn't want you to let it get to you," Naomi E. says. "I figured you know she's just . . . how she is. I didn't think—"

"I just wish you *would* think sometimes," I say, filling up my water bottle. I make sure to keep my voice low. "Guess what? She thought it was funny to turn ME into a costume, making fun of my hair. Think about how she thinks it's 'weird' that I'm smart. That it's 'weird' that my hair grows out of my head like this. Think about why people always ask if I'm adopted. And why that lady thought Momma was your babysitter. Think about how that makes me feel. Think about all the stuff that is happening in the world, right here in New York. I *have* to think about it; I don't have a choice. Think about how much I have to think about how to *be*, and stop telling me just 'be myself' like it's this easy thing."

She looks like I've slapped her.

"It's . . . sometimes, instead of making fun of me for watching the news or talking about protests or doing all my weekend homework on Friday, or . . . everything. Just think about something other than yourself just once."

"Wait, what?" she says. "When I make fun of you for watching the news, I'm teasing, you know, like sisters do? Or like I thought sisters do? Kind of the way you make fun of me all the time for being lazy? I don't get how that's different."

"No. You really don't. Sometimes I don't even know if you see me. Like, really *see* me. I. Am. Black. And *I* think that's a good thing. But sometimes it seems like a big part of the world doesn't. Do you ever think about that? Momma talks about how you have to adjust and how hard it is because your mom was gone for so long and you never had sisters before and you're not used to anything. We have to tiptoe around you and be considerate about everything. I know you've been an only child all your life, but so is Gigi and *she's* not selfish. She understands. *She* cares."

"How am I supposed to understand the way Gigi does?" says Naomi E. "Don't you think it's hard for me to figure this out, to not say the wrong thing?"

"It shouldn't be that hard! I mean, look at the school we're in. Look at Mari Copeny or Naomis like Naomi Wadler!

Look at what's happening right now where we are. Remember the workshop? Look at who's in pain and who has power! I mean, even the *second graders* are having conversations about justice."

"No justice, no peace," says Bri softly. "Are you okay, Naomis?"

"No," we both say. And it's not one of those fun *say-the-same-thing* times. Yes, AND seems impossible right now.

Momma pops her head into the kitchen. "Girls, I will meet you outside in *two* minutes," she says. She takes Bri's hand and starts to leave the kitchen, just as Tom walks in. The three of them stand kind of bunched in the doorway, like they're waiting for something to happen.

"Hey, is it time for the revolution?" Tom asks. "Are you ready to stick it to the Man?"

"*You're* kind of the Man," I say. "And I don't mean that in the hip-hop way." He looks a little surprised, so I add, "No offense."

"That's pretty good, actually," he says, and smiles.

"Dad, can I talk to you?" Naomi E. says loudly.

"Sure," he says, and they go into the living room and start talking in low voices.

"You okay, sweetie pie?" says Momma, patting my shoulder. "That was a little . . ." She trails off.

"It was just a joke; I'll apologize if I was rude," I mumble. But I'm pretty sure I won't.

"Not rude, exactly, but you didn't seem that joke-y either," says Momma. She laughs a little. "Tom's right—it *was* a good one."

I look up. "Really?"

"Sure, I mean . . . Tom's as vanilla as ice cream." Momma laughs. "Good thing I like vanilla!"

"And you like the swirl too," says Brianna, adding more baby carrots to her lunch. Momma laughs.

"What's so funny?" Bri asks.

"Never mind," I say, shaking my head, and wishing I could laugh too.

"Momma always gets the vanilla-and-chocolate swirl when we get Mister Softee," says Bri, looking confused. "It's true!"

"Momma, I think I need another walk soon," I say. "Bri can come too," I add quickly, before she can say anything. "But just Bri. Like the old days. I'm not trying to be mean; I just . . . need *us* for a little while."

Momma hugs us both to her. "You're not okay, are you?" she asks.

"No," I say. "I'm not."

CHAPTER THIRTY-TWO

Naomi E.

On the train, my stomach's swirling and my head hurts and I know if I try to make one word come out of my mouth, I will burst into tears.

I had no idea Naomi Marie thought all those awful things about me.

The stuff she said—about who's in pain and who has power. I need time. I need a dictionary. I need someone to help me through this, because it's a double whammy of feeling so awful that I hurt her without knowing and worry that I don't really understand how eleven-year-old me is supposed to take on these big ideas I've never even thought about.

She said I should stop making fun of her for the extra things she does, like watching the news, or practicing for a spelling bee that hasn't even been announced yet. I thought teasing is what sisters do. But like with every single thing I ever thought, apparently, I was wrong.

Brianna reaches for my hand. There's comfort in the warmth of her little hand in mine. I appreciate the show of friendship, but she's just pulling me off the C. I didn't realize we were at Hoyt-Schermerhorn.

From the time we're on the G to when we reach our stop and start walking to school, I remember that whenever things get hard, my mother says to take it one day at a time. But I'm more in one-second-at-a-time territory. I can't think ahead even five minutes.

When we get near school, I look up and realize Naomi Marie and Brianna have been walking ahead of me. The minute I step into the building, I realize I cannot do this. I cannot be here. I must be really desperate, because school bathrooms are the worst place that exists, but I head straight there and hide in a stall. I wish I could get the crying out, but it's stuck inside. I feel numb.

I flush, in case anyone notices I was in there awhile, and wash my hands; and instead of heading to my locker, I go to the nurse's office. A woman at a desk looks up. I should have thought about this. But then I remember, whenever Jenelle threw up last year, she got sent home.

"I threw up," I say, lying to the face of this nurse whose name I don't even know.

"Ew," she says, which doesn't seem like a very medical response. "Have a seat. I'm Cindy. I don't think we've met."

"Naomi Woods," I say.

"I'm good with blood, even with broken bones. But I have work to do with gastrointestinal distress."

I have no idea what she's talking about. "Can you call my mom to come get me?" I ask.

"Are you in pain?" she asks.

I nod. At least that's the truth.

"Let's find your sheet and then we'll give her a call," she says.

"The one named Sarah is my mom," I say. The thought of her calling Valerie now is just— I need my mom.

"Okay, here we go. Is this the number?" she asks, showing me what's printed on the sheet. "Why don't you go sit behind that curtain. There's a bathroom there if you need it. And if you need it, please be sure you get there in time." She smiles.

It's almost an hour before my mother shows up. She puts her hand on my forehead, then both hands on my cheeks. "Let's go," she says after she signs me out. "Did Brianna bring home a stomach bug?" she asks.

I shake my head.

"Is anyone else sick? Do you think it's something you ate?"

I shake my head, but I'm not sure she sees—she's using her

phone to get an Uber.

The car comes pretty quickly. We sit in the back, and she reaches for something in one of her big bags. "If you throw up," she says, handing me a plastic bag from Target, "do it in here."

I nod, a solid dose of guilt mixing in with all the other feelings.

When we finally get to her apartment, we settle at the tiny kitchen-table-for-two. "Did you really throw up?" she asks.

I shake my head. "I'm sorry. I couldn't be there. I had this huge . . . Actually, *I* didn't really have anything. But Naomi Marie let me have it this morning. She said I was selfish and didn't care about her and I only think about myself and I have no idea what it's like to be her, how she can't just be herself and how could I have done all that and not even known it?"

And all of a sudden, tears are pouring and my nose is stuffed up and disgusting. Mom reaches for a tissue box and puts it in front of me. Then she stands next to me and rubs circles on my back, like she used to at night when I couldn't sleep.

"I'm pretty sure I'll be crying for the rest of my life, just so you know," I say. "Can I *please* live here with you?" Really, it's the only solution. There's no way through that mess with Naomi Marie. I can't do anything right. I don't get which things are friendly teasing and which hurt her feelings. "She says I don't know what everything is like for her, how our lives are different because we're different colors. I believe her, I believe it's different, but she sees it so clearly and I don't."

Mom sits back down so she's looking at me, but I kind of wish she could do that *and* back circles—her hand rubbing my back makes me feel better, the comfort of being little and knowing someone will help you, no matter what. But then I remember the times Naomi Marie has talked about my comfort like it's a bad thing.

I never ask my mom to live with her because I know it hurts her that I can't, because she has a ridiculous schedule and wouldn't be home most of the hours I'd be home. But I'm too miserable to worry about her feelings. "I'm old enough to be okay home alone," I say. "Or I could come to the theater or whatever and do my homework there."

"It's not possible. And we should talk about how to work through whatever's going on, not run away from it."

Maybe I should have stayed at school.

"What was it about this morning, with Naomi Marie? What really happened?"

"I don't even know how it started. All of a sudden she was listing all these things she can't stand about me. Like she said it's wrong or bad or whatever that I tell her to be herself, because . . . I don't really know. It had something to do with her being black, and how I don't get what that's like for her.

"She also said I don't care enough about the news and that I'm selfish because I don't think about what it feels like when people assume Valerie is my nanny or whatever. And what I assume is, those people are idiots! What else could I assume? Aren't we supposed to not care about insults from people we don't respect? And . . ." The tears build up again and I have to stop.

After an impressive nose blow, I say, "And she wishes I'd talk but how can I know which of the things I might say will upset her? Like she got annoyed at this girl for saying someone was her spirit animal, which I didn't know wasn't okay to say. That's the thing. If I really have to live there, I'm never going to talk again because it's like random bombs go off. I don't know how to know what will offend her. I don't know how to live with her. I don't know how not to disappoint her every stupid minute of the day."

Mom stands and pulls me into a tight hug. And I wouldn't want to offend Valerie or my dad, but there's nothing that comes close to a mom's hug. "A lot of this is on your dad and me," she says softly. "Naomi Marie is right that these issues *are* things we need to talk about, and we didn't talk about it enough. I kept thinking, *Maybe when she's older.* That's why I was glad you were doing all those workshops. Didn't that give you some kind of background or understanding or . . ."

I think back to the summer of workshops. "It was a lot of information, all at once. I tried to pay attention. I mean, I did, but it was kind of like school. Or maybe it was like when we did yoga with Myla, remember?"

She looks at me like that makes no sense.

"How we thought, *Now that we learned this and know how to do it, we're going to do it all the time?*" Mom nods. We both know that her yoga mat is buried under three shows' worth of costume scraps.

"There's no easy answer," Mom says. "But no one starts out knowing everything. Every—"

I cut her off. "That's the thing, though. Naomi Marie DOES. She knows everything."

"I'm sorry, but I don't believe that's true." She looks at her phone. "I do believe that *you* believe it, though. But Naomi, you have to remember that having a lot to learn isn't a bad thing. Learn. Make the effort. Don't be afraid to make mistakes."

I almost burst into tears again. "But when I make mistakes, she's so disappointed and it's awful!"

"No one expected this to be simple. It's a hard thing to merge two families. But I'm sure Naomi Marie will be reasonable. Maybe ask her questions to fill in the holes of the things you don't know?"

I think about the day when I sat and read Brianna's picture books, the ones with black people on the cover. I remember thinking they were beautiful, but not familiar—not just that they were new books to me. There was something about the stories themselves that felt different. I always thought of picture books as comfort food. But this was more like . . . a really nice kind of gentle learning.

"Are you going to be okay?" Mom asks.

I shrug. I know Mom has costume work to do.

I rest my head on the kitchen table.

CHAPTER THIRTY-THREE

Naomi Marie

My stomach is jumpy all day at school; I'm not sorry about what I said to Naomi E., but I'm very sorry that she had that frozen look on her face, like she was lost and had no idea how to get back home. Is this like Jen? I mean, she's my sister, so I can't give up, but . . . *am* I supposed to teach her? Is it different this time?

Do I have to ask myself all the questions? What if I don't really want answers?

I wonder what I'm going to say to her when I see her in Creative Writing, but it turns out that I don't have to say anything: Tricia Hightower says she saw Naomi E. leaving with "her real mom" during first period. Jen laughs when she says that; I ignore them both. Before I can ask to call Momma, I get a text from her saying that Naomi E.'s mom picked her up early because she wasn't feeling well. I stand outside the Creative Writing classroom to text Naomi E. "**Hope you feel better**" with a period instead of an exclamation point. Everything feels like one big question mark, though.

"Put that away NOW," says a voice behind me, and I jump. It's Carla.

"I'm sorry, I—"

"You know the rules—no phones during the day. You come to the office if you need to make a call or communicate with your family. Please put it away and keep it there."

"I just had to—" I start, but she's gone. Great. So much for asking if I can talk to her about Wacky Hat/Hair Day. She probably won't even let me into her office now. She probably thought I was playing a game on my phone. She probably thinks I'm a Girl Trying to Game the System, but not in the good way that Julie would have been proud of. She probably thinks I don't care about my grades, or being an example for my sisters, or that my momma maybe losing her job because there's no more funding, or Daddy being lonely, or how to have more than one best friend, or anything important. She probably thinks I'm . . . frivolous. And while that's a very good word, it's not one that I want describing me.

This is just great.

In Creative Writing, the "do-now" writing prompt should be a breeze. There's so much I need to work through! I start with a list, like always:

> Figuring out what to say to Naomi E.
>
> Going to Shelly Ann's more (and maybe today)
>
> Setting people like Jen straight!
>
> Having both Gigi and Xio as best friends without making either one of them feel bad
>
> Thinking of Gruber as not quite an enemy, but not quite a friend . . . like a halfway decent frenemy?
>
> Telling Naomi E. the truth without making her feel bad
>
> Telling Naomi E. that her feeling bad isn't the point
>
> Also going to Morningstar for those mint chocolate chip cookies
>
> Being a good Reading Buddy, which means making sure the words I give Waverly mean something, and not just to me
>
> Telling Naomi E. the truth without making *me* feel bad

Even though we have a double period of Creative Writing, I could keep going. This is just like, a start.

I add one more.

Accepting that even though Naomi E. is my sister, she'll
never be my *sister*

Then I cross that one out. It looks too harsh on paper.
Even though it's true.
Is it?
Definitely sometimes.
But does it always have to be?
We started out so far apart, and now we

Laugh together when Bri does something silly
Share eye rolls when the parents do something even sil-
lier (which is all the time)
Share eye rolls when somebody asks if one of us is
adopted
Pretend that people don't usually think it's me
Try to figure out impossible things like why Gruber is
so annoying
Play board games
Play chess
And checkers
And checssers, which is a game we made up out of both
Need privacy sometimes
Cry together secretly in the bathroom when we get
in trouble at school, which has never happened
to me in my life and I'm so embarrassed and

worried that now Carla will just think bad things about me forever

"Five more minutes!" calls out Katherine.

Uh-oh. I go back to my solo list of things I need to work out:

> Not crying alone because I wonder if Carla will only think bad things about me because I'm the Black Naomi
> Ignoring people like Jen who are trying to "quench my spirit," the way Kevin always says at the end of youth group meetings
> Going to youth group more—they have good snacks
> Figuring out how to go to youth group without sitting through the boring service
> Figuring out how to help my community
> Figuring out what my community is
> Figuring out who *I* am

I don't want to turn in this list. I know we can write personal stuff that Katherine won't share, but this is more than personal, it's private. I've got two minutes to do something else that I can turn in, before I add loser-who-didn't-do-the-assignment to my list. And let Katherine down.

I look at the homework prompt up on the Smart Board:

Can you point to a time in your life when you thought a certain way and then something or someone changed your thinking?

Okay, that's not happening right now. What can I do? Six-word memoir. That's easy. Go!

I put my head down on my desk. I'm tired of explaining myself. To everyone.

"Where's Naomi E.?" says Bri when we meet in the yard at dismissal.

"She's having a special date with her mom today," says Momma. "So I thought we'd have a special date too. And dessert for dinner—at Shelly Ann's!"

"Yay!" says Bri, dancing around us in a little circle.

"Salad later," says Momma. "Of course."

"Is she feeling better?" I ask. "Naomi E.? And, um, can we get going?"

"Yes, yes, I know, not cool to have your momma around," says Momma. "Especially when I do this—" She gives me a big kiss on the cheek in front of everyone, including DeVante Swing, who just has to be right there. He waves. "And yes, she's fine. Just having a little extra mom time. Which is what we're going to have right now too."

Shelly Ann has just baked a fresh caramel cake, and it smells like love, which I feel like I need so much right now I could cry. Momma gets us each our own slice, and we have lemonade instead of water.

"Is today a special day?" asks Brianna. "Or are we having an As a Black Woman talk? We haven't had one in a loooong time, and I'll be six soon! Or did I do something extra good?"

Or does Momma think I did something extra bad? I wonder. I know Naomi E. talked to Tom about what I said to her. And that means Tom probably told Momma. I look up at Momma to see if she has Disappointed Face. She smiles at me, but it's one of those sad-eyed serious smiles, so I can't tell if I'm in trouble.

Bri starts telling us about how Yesenia called her Scaredy Squirrel, and how she gave Travis seven "put-ups" even though he cries during rest time. Then Nef and her mom come in, and I think it's a coincidence until Nef's mom invites Bri to sit with them, and Momma and I are left alone at our table.

"As a Black woman," she starts. Then stops and smiles again. "You know, Bri's right. We haven't had one of these in a while."

"It was different when it was just us," I say. "Not Yes, AND."

"It's hard sometimes, being a sister, isn't it?" asks Momma after a while.

I shrug. "I mean, but it's fun too." Momma looks at me

with so much love in her eyes that I take a deep breath and just say it. "It's . . . being a *sister* sister is kind of . . . complicated sometimes. I don't always know if I can be my whole self."

Momma nods. "Do you want to talk about it?"

"That's the thing," I say. "I can talk about it with *you*, but . . . how do I talk about it with Naomi E.? Without hurting her feelings? Or . . . mine?"

"Pain is a part of life," says Momma softly. "We can't avoid it, so we have to figure out how to deal with it."

"But how do we know when we're dealing with it the right way?" I ask. "Sometimes I feel like Naomi E. doesn't want to know all of me, or wants to pretend that I'm not me, and that makes me sad and angry and confused, and . . ." I trail off.

"Well, we can't always know . . . but we can reflect on our purpose—do we want to simply make the pain go away? Or do we want to make the situation that caused the pain better?"

"Sometimes I just want it to go away, to be honest," I say. "Is that bad?"

"Of course not, honey, that's real," Momma says. "But I will tell you one thing: no one else should be deciding for you whether or not you can be your whole self. That's your decision to make. But as a Black woman, I know very well that feeling—that you have to hide and conform and quench some of yourself to make other people comfortable."

"I know we talk a lot about making sure she's comfortable, and how she's not used to a lot of stuff we're used to. . . ."

"And maybe we didn't talk enough about how to do that without dimming your own light," says Momma. "Maybe we don't need to go to any more workshops."

Yeah, right, I think. And I guess it shows, because she laughs. "What I mean is, this is on us, all the parents, to help you girls navigate this. And when I think about it, even when we talk about what happens in workshops, we don't always *live* it."

"So what does that mean?" I ask.

"I'm not sure," says Momma. "But I want you to know that I don't have it all figured out. None of us do. I'm sorry to say that it doesn't get easier when you're an adult."

"Great. Thanks, Momma," I say.

"I also want you to know that I love you unconditionally. And so does Tom. And so does Naomi E. And love is a powerful thing. Never underestimate it."

"Are you guys gonna make us have a Talk?" I ask. "I know I said some things that made her upset. Because *I* was upset. And"—I look down—"I'm not sorry I said them. But . . ."

"We're not going to make you do anything. I have faith in both of you. And we will be here to support you both."

I don't really know what that means, especially since she just basically said that the adults were supposed to fix this for us. Maybe it means that they don't know how, and that feels a little scary.

But she lets me finish her cake, and Shelly Ann gives us two pieces to bring home. At least I can say "Shelly Ann sent you some cake" to Naomi E.

And we'll see how it goes from there.

CHAPTER THIRTY — FOUR

Naomi E.

My mom is really understanding and flexible, but once she makes up her mind, it's impossible to get her to change it. So even though I offer to clean her refrigerator, organize her costume bags, and vacuum the apartment, she says I have to go back to the yellow house tonight.

The whole ride over, I'm thinking I just need one more night away. I'd be happy to curl up on the couch at Mom's if she wants the bed. I'll sleep on the floor! In the bathtub! I have the worst dread-y feeling in my stomach.

At least Mom let me wait until bedtime.

When we get to the yellow house, she hugs me really

tight. "This isn't something that gets fixed instantly," she says. "But you're coming from a place of wanting to do better. And you're going to need to ask for help from your dad and Valerie navigating this. But I want you to know that even though I don't live here with you, I do, in a way. Because you carry me in your heart just like I carry you in mine. Remember—it really is okay to make mistakes, especially when you're trying to do better, even if it feels awful in that moment. I love you. Call me tomorrow and let me know how you're doing."

I don't want to let go of this hug. But then she says, "I hope you don't throw up at school again," and squeezes my arm.

It almost makes me laugh. Or not quite almost.

I'm glad it's late, because as fun as Brianna can be, I am not in the mood to be slam-hugged with "White Naomi's back! White Naomi! White Naomi!" I want to sneak into bed and deal with everything tomorrow.

As if that were a possibility.

Dad and Valerie are at the kitchen table, their hands wrapped around big green mugs. "How are you doing?" Dad asks at the same time Valerie says, "You must be wiped out."

I shrug and nod. "Just going to get ready for bed. Too tired for anything else."

"Okay," Valerie says. "We brought you something from Shelly Ann's, but it can wait."

I take a step toward my room. "What did you get? Just so I can, you know, think about it."

"Caramel cake," Valerie says with a small smile.

I step into our room, and I'm getting my pajamas when Naomi Marie walks in. "Getting ready for bed," I say. Because the pajamas and the fact that it's late wouldn't be enough clues.

I'm so out of whack that I put my pajamas on backward and don't realize it until the collar is practically keeping me from breathing. I twist the top around and brush my teeth quickly and walk into our room, which is already dark.

I pull back the covers and climb in under the soft, snuggly blanket.

Naomi Marie and Valerie are wrapping up their every-night routine on Naomi Marie's bed, so I face the wall to give them as much privacy as possible in a shared room.

Valerie stands and I hear her blowing me a kiss before she closes the door.

I'm waiting. And then I realize I'm waiting and it's not fair that it's always Naomi Marie who has to start the hard conversations. "We should probably talk," I say.

"Okay."

"I'm sorry," I say. Because that's a good place to start.

She doesn't say anything. I know she wonders if my apology is the right kind and I want it to be. I hope it is.

"I've been thinking about all the stuff you said this

morning. I know that I have a lot to learn. And I'm try-ing. But I want to maybe warn you that I can't suddenly know everything at once. I know that's probably obvious, but I'm saying it because if I make mistakes and say things that hurt your feelings, or ask questions that show how little I know, it's not because I'm not trying. I always want to have your back and support you and be a good sister. It just means knowing so much more than I ever realized."

I hear her fluff her pillow and sit up. "I'm glad you want to do better," she says, in what I think of as her teacher voice. "And I'm sorry you felt so sick that you had to leave school."

I sit up too. Sleep won't be here for a long time, and I'd bet that Dad and Valerie will not be knocking on the door, telling us to stop talking. They want this to be better too. "I really did have a stomachache, but I told the nurse I threw up and I didn't, so she'd call my mom."

Instead of gasping and calling me a liar, which I might expect from someone who seems so school-perfect (even though I'm not supposed to think that, but I don't really get why since it seems like she's *trying* to be school-perfect), she says, "You can still be hurtful when you're trying. And I need to tell you when that happens. But I'm glad you're try-ing. Also, I'm glad you got some time with your mom."

"Thank you," I say. Even though it's a small thing, it seems important to be careful. We're in a kind of tender place.

"I know we can't figure it all out tonight," I say, "but part of what has me feeling scared of hurting you or making you mad is the way you say that if I care about things, then I'd learn about them, because I think I do care, but I don't really know *how* to learn about . . . everything. It feels so big and I have no idea where or how to start. I sometimes want to tell you I'm only eleven. But then I remember you are too."

"Yes, *and*," she says, and it almost sounds like she might be smiling, "I don't have everything all figured out."

"Right," I say. "It sure looks like you do."

"I promise, I don't," she says.

I only half believe that. "You know a lot more than I do, and I think you might not get that I don't . . . think as fast as you maybe? I'm trying, but I have so much more to learn and that makes me nervous, because I know you're impatient for me to be someone I'm not yet."

She's quiet. But it's not the kind you worry about sinking into like quicksand.

"I want you to be who you are," she finally says, "but one who sees all of me, not just the parts that are easy."

"I'm trying," I say. Even though I don't know what this kind of trying looks like. But I do know it's something I have to do.

CHAPTER THIRTY - FIVE

Naomi Marie

The next morning, me and Naomi E. just talk about easy stuff while we wait on the subway platform at Hoyt-Schermerhorn, like how my dog (well, my dad's dog) really did eat my homework last week but I did it over anyway because who would ever believe that, and how she's going to use peer mediation strategies to low-key not letting Gruber get to her without being all-out mean. We wait a long time, and there are a bunch of train announcements, but we can't understand anything they're saying through the loudspeaker. It sounds something like "THRUAT W$Y? HVNQ B?TQVIFJ. IHEVITEO ORVGJNGIRIEPJXXWHRHE."

"Are they speaking English?" asks Bri.

"Nope," says Naomi E. "But it doesn't matter. Whatever they're saying, it means we're going to be LATE."

I think for a minute. "Should we try the bus?"

"If we want to get to school next week, sure," says Naomi E.

"Ha-ha," I say. Just then, the G train pulls in, and I grab Bri's hand tight because the car is super packed with grumpy commuters. The three of us squeeze on, and the doors shut, just missing this guy's backpack. A baby starts crying.

Then, an announcement: "Due to an earlier incident, this train will end at Hoyt-Schermerhorn. No passengers after Hoyt-Schermerhorn. This train is out of service." The train starts, stops, and the doors open.

Uh-oh.

"I hate that," says Naomi E. "What's an 'earlier incident'? A bank robbery? A flash mob? They should really explain more than that."

"So you do think it's important to have all the info some-times," I say, but I'm smiling. She rolls her eyes, but nods and smiles back.

"What should we do?" she asks when we get off.

"We have to take the F!" says Brianna. We look at her. "That's what the lady said."

"Okay, I don't know how you know that, but I think you're right. I think if we take the G train back toward Queens, then transfer at Bedford Nostrand to an F, we'll be on the right track. Hey! 'track,' get it?"

"No," says Naomi E.

"Should we text Momma and double-check?" I say.

"Probably," says Naomi E. "But . . ."

"But it would be so much cooler if we just did it on our own, right?" I ask. "And then later we can just tell her and Tom casually and they'll be like *You're so mature!* And we'll get smartphones."

"I don't know about that," says Naomi E. "My dad told me last week that they were thinking of taking our dumb phones away and getting us pagers."

"I don't even know what that means," I say.

"Me either, but it sounds old-school enough to be really embarrassing," says Naomi E. "But yeah, let's just figure it out ourselves. At least we can show that we're more grown-up than they give us credit for."

"I know! We may get Shelly Ann's and Morningstar!" I say. "Or we can just get Morningstar . . . since we had Shelly Ann's yesterday."

"*Now* you're talking," she replies.

"You guys are talking so much we missed the train," says Bri.

"Ooops," I say. "We'll get the next one."

The next one turns out to be a J train. Huh?

"Plot twist!" says Naomi E. We get on since it doesn't seem like we have a choice, and it takes us to the Lower East Side.

"If you take me to Katz's, I won't tell on you," says Bri. "But I get my own pastrami sandwich."

"We're not going to Katz's, and there's nothing to tell," I say through clenched teeth. I'm trying not to show that I'm nervous.

"But we're at the Katz's stop," says Bri. "Are you lost?"

"No!" Naomi E. and I both say really loudly. "We're just . . . turned around."

"I'm hungry," says Bri.

It takes three more trains and a trip to Williamsburg before we get to school. And we are really, really late. As soon as we walk into school, Bri runs to her classroom. We watch her go in before we start to head to ours.

"What period is this?" asks Naomi E.

"I have no idea," I answer. Then Mark, the assistant principal, comes out of his office and sees us.

"Naomis! Where have you been? Your parents called thirty minutes ago. Apparently you were not answering your phones?"

"Our phones were off," I say. "We're not supposed to have them on unless it's an emergency."

"Not coming straight to school constitutes an emergency," says Mark. "You're in middle school now; you have to be responsible."

"We were trying to be!" says Naomi E. "We—"

Mark holds up his hand. "Just go sign in at the office and

call your parents," he says, and stomps off.

"I don't think we're getting Shelly Ann's or Morningstar," I say.

At lunch, Gigi and I decide to head up to the library, and a couple of the other Reading Buddies who hung with us last time kind of follow us, and then some other people decide to come along, which makes me feel like I have a squad! A pretty nerdy one, but I'll take it.

Daisuke doesn't look that glad to see our lunch-carrying squad. "I'm trusting you guys" is all he says. "And I'm ready for you." He smiles and points to a rolling cart piled with books. "Social justice explosion!"

"What snacks do you have?" asks Gruber, who I didn't realize had come in behind us.

"We're here to talk books, not snacks, Gruber," I say. "So if you're not down with that, you know where you can go."

"Sorry," he mutters. And stays. *Well, well, well.*

"What is reading all these books supposed to *do*?" asks Alyssa. "Also, nice shirt."

I look down at my Black Girls Code top. It *is* a nice shirt, so I just say "Thank you."

"I mean, I think we *are* doing something," says Gigi slowly. "I like reading and talking about books like this." A lot of people nod. "I think it's helping. At least me, it is."

"What do you mean?" I ask.

"I mean, I sort of knew about Malala Yousafzai before, but it was different when I read her book," says Gigi. "It . . . opened my eyes and inspired me at the same time."

"It made me scared," says Ifeoma. "Like, I can't even imagine living in her world."

"But you can imagine it now that you read the book," says Gigi. "That's the thing."

"That one about Barbara Rose Johns was awesome," says DJ. "She was almost the same age as us!"

"What was that about?" asks Gruber.

"This girl who didn't like how her segregated school was so bad, and she got all the kids to go on strike, and it started a whole movement and court case, and— Here, I'm finished with it. You can check it out next."

"Cool," says Gruber. And he actually takes the book! And *then* he recommends *York*, which of course I already read, but I pretend that I haven't, and it's awesome anyway.

Everyone starts talking about all the books they've read, and how they made them feel. Alyssa says that she loved *The Real Boy*, so Ifeoma tells her to read *The Girl Who Drank the Moon* next. But Aunjalique recommends *A Long Walk to Water*, and they're off arguing like Alyssa will only be able to read one more book, ever, for the rest of her life.

Gigi comes over to me.

"Did we just start a club?" I ask. "Like, without even trying to?"

"Maybe," she says, "a book club that's about more than books. It's like—"

"Not just *reading* books, but *living* them in a way," I say slowly. "Figuring out how others' stories can help us write our own." I sound like Katherine. And Momma. Well, not the Momma who is probably going to have a lot to say about our train escapade this morning.

"Uh, you sound like a teacher," Gigi says. "Try to keep that to yourself. I kind of want to imagine that we're just a bunch of cool kids. Not doing *experiential learning* or whatever."

"Book learning is in my blood," I say, in a fake-deep voice. "Haven't you seen my library card catalog sweatshirt?"

"What's a card catalog?"

I look around again. People will probably think we're just library nerds who get eating-upstairs privileges, and I guess we are, but I'm liking what being a library nerd means. We care.

"I have an idea." I raise my voice a little. "Let's make a list of ways we can get more people talking just like this."

And we start there.

CHAPTER THIRTY - SIX

Naomi E.

Why do I feel guilty? Why do I keep thinking about how, on the phone, I kept telling Dad that we really came straight to school, it's just that we had to take so many trains? I sounded guilty even to me, and I know I didn't do anything wrong. Dad says they were really worried and we're going to review all the rules at dinner and we should leave earlier tomorrow. Which isn't exactly news.

I'm kind of zombying through the morning, head down, trying to survive until my next class. I guess Edie notices, because when I'm at my locker between periods, she grabs me by the arm and says, "You're here? Hey, are you okay?"

"Yeah," I say. And when I look at her, it's so nice to see a friendly face that I stop what I'm doing and smile at her.

"You didn't answer my texts yesterday. Were you sick? When you missed Advisory again today I figured you were really still out, feeling awful."

"I sort of was," I say. Which is true. "I'll fill you in at lunch."

She nods. "Glad you're feeling better," she says.

In truth, I'm still shaky about whether things are okay between Naomi Marie and me, but it's a long walk to Harris's classroom and I'd better get going.

I didn't need to rush. Harris isn't here and the classroom is chaos and my brain feels like it might be infected or on fire. THIS classroom is like one of those books with no adults, and kids gone completely wild.

"Gruber, at your desk. Now," Harris says, walking into the room five minutes late.

"It's not like you were ready when class started," Gruber mutters, loud enough that Harris hears him. Harris shakes his head. It's only November, but it's like teachers all think: *Gruber.*

"As you know," Harris says, leaning against the front of his desk, "today we evaluate how peer mediation is going, how we're doing." He makes a face and reaches behind him and seems surprised to find what looks like a tennis trophy in his hand. "Does this belong . . . Never mind. Onward. I

259

want to hear about what you've been doing. What's working. What's not. Any suggestions for improvement. Let's respect the anonymity of those who've used our services by using fake names in place of actual names."

Some of us look confused, so Harris keeps talking. "You've been acting like such pros, I've forgotten this is new to you. You can simply say, 'Martin approached us with a conflict he was having with Jane regarding respect for personal space.' Let's pull our desks into a circle and get started."

The squeak of desk and chair on school floor is right up there with chalk on a chalkboard, and of course it takes longer than it should because someone, whose name begins with G and ends with *ruber*, decides that he needs to be able to see the clock but then decides it's more important to be near Harris's desk so he can check out that random tennis trophy.

"Who wants to begin?" Harris asks.

Ronak and Sayantani raise their hands in that gross, pick-ME-not-HER way. Harris looks for someone else to call on. This kid I don't really know named Aram has his hand half raised, like he plans to pull it right back down if Harris looks his way, but Harris sees him and says, "Aram, remind me who your partners were."

For some reason Aram stands. "I have been partners with Sayantani and Yaakov. The mediation I want to talk about was when I was partners with Yaakov."

Everyone turns to look at Yaakov. "Really?" Yaakov says. "That chicken thing?"

"It was interesting, wasn't it?" Amar says.

Yaakov shrugs.

Aram says, "Basically, this kid, I mean, Jane?, came to us to complain that she was being treated in an unfriendly way by, um, lots of Martins?"

Harris nods. "Sounds about normal for kindergarten."

Now Yaakov is standing too. "Does it sound normal if that bunch of Martins was actually a bunch of chickens?" He sits back down.

Everyone laughs.

"I beg your pardon?" Harris says.

Amar says, "It's true. The kindergarten students were introduced to the chickens last month and Soph—I mean Jane—said that all the chickens were *buck-buck*ing around, um, the other Martins and Janes, but when our Jane wanted to interact with the chickens, they ran away. Jane said it really hurt her feelings."

Everyone is smiling or laughing and shaking their heads.

"What did you do?" Gruber asks. "Did you sit down with Jane and the chickens, and work it out by listening and asking open-ended questions and summarizing the chickens' feelings?"

I'm surprised he remembers all the important peer mediation pointers. Also, that's kind of a funny question, Gruber. I try to smile at him, but my face doesn't let me.

Yaakov stands again and says, "I told Jane to talk to her teacher. I thought it was out of our, I can't think of the word, but that it wasn't possible to peer mediate between different species."

Everyone laughs again.

"So that was . . . different," Harris says. "Who would like to share next?"

Sayantani talks about stopping a fight during a wall-ball game gone bad. Sawyer tells a long story about someone writing in another kid's notebook. I'm drifting off, not in an actual sleep way—more like my brain is resting. Which, of course, leads Harris to ask, "Naomi E., Gruber, I haven't heard from you."

Gruber stands like he's about to give a speech. What is it with standing in this class? "Easy stuff," he says. "I nailed it."

"Would you like to provide a few more details?" Harris asks without much kindness in his voice. Gruber's silent. "Naomi E., what about you? Do you think it's been easy stuff?"

My head's shaking no before I even have a chance to think about how I want to respond. "It's not what I thought it would be," I say, hoping maybe that's enough and it can be someone else's turn.

"Talk some more about that," Harris says.

"I thought we were going to help solve other kids' problems."

"Isn't that what you did?" Harris stands and walks over to Gruber and, without taking his eyes off me, grabs the tennis trophy out of Gruber's hands.

"Not really," I say. "I thought people would feel better, like relieved, when we were done. Or that we'd come up with compromises that really made both people happy. And I don't feel like we made anyone happy."

"Speak for yourself," Gruber says.

"I AM!" I shout. "Sorry."

Harris's eyes get wide at my shout, but he doesn't say anything.

Ronak raises his hand and Harris nods at him. "But who feels good right after an argument? I don't."

People kind of shrug and nod.

"I guess," I say. "But you know how when there's no great solution, we tell them to do rock/paper/scissors? It's not that, I don't know, rewarding? I can do everything I'm supposed to do—ask open-ended questions, listen and repeat back, have them say how they're feeling and try to come up with a compromise; and in the end, we tell them there's no way to solve their problem so they should make some random decision? It feels like we're failing."

I look around the room, and it seems like some people agree with me. Ronak's nodding, and Sayantani looks to Harris, maybe waiting to hear what he thinks.

"But the purpose of peer mediation," Harris says, now holding the tennis trophy, "isn't all solution focused. It's to help other students, especially younger students, learn how to settle their arguments and fights. We want to give them those tools so that when mediators are not available, they'll know what to do."

I think about Mariah and Elle, the girls who fought when they were playing tag. I doubt our mediation changed anything. And I don't think I gave them anything useful for next time. And maybe I only made things worse between Emma and Waverly. When I think of Prisha, though, I remember that she spoke up for herself. Which is hard to do.

"Does that make sense, Naomi E.?" Harris says. He looks down at his hands, shakes his head fast, and opens the closet and puts the trophy in there.

"Yes," I say, even though what I mean is that I still need to think more about it.

I'm going to need three lifetimes to do all the thinking I need to do.

CHAPTER THIRTY — SEVEN

Naomi Marie

I'm sitting in Creative Writing thinking of Waverly and Emma and how sometimes people don't see who you are because they aren't looking closely enough, and sometimes we don't see each other because we think we already know what we look like. How Gruber can be so annoying and halfway decent at the same time. How I want Naomi E. to see the whole me *and* be her true self.

I look at the prompt again:

Can you point to a time in your life when you thought a certain way and then something or someone changed your thinking?

Usually by now I'd be on my second draft of my Creative Writing assignment, but I've been in the list-making phase for days. So many things and people have *changed my thinking*!

Daddy, when he told me it would be fun to have a baby sister (I'll never tell Bri, though)

The movie *Akeelah and the Bee*

Cheese popcorn and caramel popcorn mixed together

Being called Naomi Marie

The book *A Ring of Endless Light*

Living a *Yes, and* life

The book *Brown Girl Dreaming*

Every time I hear Dr. Neil DeGrasse Tyson talk about something I think is going to be boring

The book of Luke

Also the story of Esther

That time when Jenn Harlow said she heard I cheated in Girls Gaming the System

That time I finished Jenn's and Orchid's wampum belts for them and they got credit. Stole it, really

That time Mr. Mack should have realized that I did all the work, because seriously, really???!!

Whoa. I'm getting way off track here. What made me even think of that stuff in the first place?

Wishing Naomi E. would say something about who I
    am, but then living smack in the middle of *be*
    careful what you wish for
Wondering if Naomi E. really didn't mean to say some-
    thing about who I am, and if it matters if she
    meant it or not
Wondering if liking to be a leader *sometimes* (okay, most of
    the time) has to mean being a teacher all the time
Wondering how to figure out where I stand when what
    I really want to do most is lie down and pull the
    covers over my head
Making a list that's helpful instead of this random list of
    I don't even know

I carefully tear these pages out of my Writer's Notebook
and fold them into a thick but small square. I put it in the
front of my jeans pocket. This goes under the "Private, not
just personal" category.

I look at the clock: five minutes until the period ends. Not
enough time to make a new list before the bell rings.

But still, I start. Because this one's not going to be for me.
I can't answer all my own questions right now, but I know
one thing I can do for Waverly.

When there is no DeVante Swing but actual okra at the salad
bar, I understand that the universe really is plotting against

me, no matter what Dr. Tyson says. So I'm not even surprised at recess when Jennifer and her squad march over. She stops and sits right next to me. "Hey," she says, like we were just texting each other heart emojis. Her crew is smiling behind her, but they don't look that into it. It must be exhausting to be friends with Jen. "I've been thinking about everything, and I'm sorry if you were offended."

Whoa. It's not a very good one, but it's actually kind of an apology. I raise my eyebrows.

"Oh-kay . . . ," I say. "So, um . . . what are you sorry about exactly?"

She laughs nervously. "I mean, the wig and all that, you know. . . . I'm not wearing it, by the way." Her minions offer up halfhearted giggles. "Guys!" she says, turning to them. "I'm serious! I didn't mean anything bad. How was I supposed to know?"

Maybe she is sorry. She's smirking, but maybe she's just trying to look cool. I look again at Jen, trying to figure out whether she's sincere or just setting me up to take me down, or what. And then I realize: Jen is not my job.

"Good question," I say. And leave it at that.

"Is that it?" Jen says. "Like, I seriously don't get all this politically correct stuff, and—"

"I don't know what you mean by 'politically correct,'" I say.

"I mean, I don't have time to get into all this stuff," she says. "I have a lot on my mind. And I'm admitting that I don't exactly know everything. So *you* tell me. Tell me why it's so bad."

"You're right." I say, standing. "You don't know everything. And neither do I." I stop. I don't have to pretend to be somebody else, or prove anything to anyone, especially not Upchuckiffer Bile.

"Okay, but like, remember how you got all mad about spirit animal? We had that Lenape unit in fifth grade, but they didn't teach us that. Like, am I supposed to travel back in time to find Native Americans to teach me all this stuff? That's a lot of work."

"Google is your friend," I say. "So is a good librarian. And knowing *actual people* who have different life experiences from you." Yikes, I really do sound like Momma. "If you really care that much. It's not my job to teach you not to be ignorant. And racist."

"Oh my God," whispers a Jenette.

"And by the way, you don't actually have to 'travel back in time' to get to know a First Nations person," I continue.

Jen is just staring at me, so I stare back. And I raise my eyebrow, just one, *perfectly*, the way I've been practicing for months! The bell rings.

"Do the work," I say. "We've been learning that since the first day of school."

CHAPTER THIRTY-EIGHT

Naomi E.

I usually stay over at Mom's on Saturday night, and by the time I get home on Sunday, everyone's in their lazy-day clothes (even though Dad and I are the only lazy ones who live here).

But Mom's friend Myla was visiting from Los Angeles, and last night was the only time they could get together, so I stayed here in the yellow house. And now everyone except me is getting dressed like they're going to a party, and it's hard not to feel like I'm not invited. Which makes no sense, because they're getting ready for church and I don't go to church.

Brianna steps into the living room and twirls in her yellow summer dress until Valerie makes her change. Naomi Marie decides she needs to write some ideas down before she forgets, and Brianna, now in her purple dress, taps her foot.

The minute they leave, I decide to get that Creative Writing homework finished. Katherine assigned it the day I went home sick, and I had just a few days to get it done.

Can you point to a time in your life when you thought a certain way and then something or someone changed your thinking?

I sit on my bed, notebook open. My first thought is peach ice cream.

I wouldn't even taste it because fruit in ice cream is gross and sometimes too frozen, but Grandpa insisted and then it became my favorite, but just for a month. (No. Too babyish. Also, impossible to "reflect" on.)

Okay, something more important. Oh! Until third grade I really liked school, but then in fourth I had Ms. Misher, who was both hard and really moody, and that changed my mind about school. No, probably not a good idea to let a teacher know I don't like school.

Sometimes it's easier to write when it's not tied up with feelings. I know! I used to think cats were disgusting—they step in a litter box where they do nasty stuff and then you might find them on your kitchen counter! But when I met

Myla's cats, I fell in love with one of them. Ketchup. (No. I am not going to write a memoir about Ketchup.)

Maybe I'm so bad at this because I'm hungry. I'm about to see what we have in the kitchen when I have the genius idea that Dad should take me to Morningstar, where I hardly get to go anymore. We could pick up croissants and bagels and some sweet stuff for later.

"So Dad," I say. He's lounging on the couch.

He puts his tablet down and meets my eyes. "This is about food, am I right? Want me to make you something?"

On what planet? Brianna is a better cook than he is. It's possible that Naomi Marie's dad's new dog, Luke Cage, is a better cook than Dad. "I thought we could stop by Morningstar on the way to Mom's. Buy some stuff I could bring her, and maybe you could bring some back here." I smile, thinking about texting Naomi Marie that there'll be a tasty treat waiting for her.

"Ask your mom. She's picking you up." Dad sits up, and I realize that he's wearing nice clothes, or at least what he thinks of as his nice clothes.

"What's up?" I ask.

"I'm joining Valerie and Naomi Marie and Brianna after church today."

"Oh, okay," I say. "Because when I saw you all dressed up, I thought maybe you were meeting them *at* church or something."

"Not today, though I would like to start going with them soon."

"Really?"

"It's important to them, and that means it's important to me, even if it has different meaning for me."

I flop onto the chair and pull the fluffy yellow pillow onto my lap. The few times I've gone to church, I always feel like everyone's engaged in doing something together, a certain dance I don't know the moves to. I don't stand at the right time or shake hands with the person behind me when I'm supposed to. I picture Dad being as confused as me at church, and I wonder if that would annoy Valerie. "Do you make mistakes with Valerie?"

"I'm sure I do," he says. "We all do."

"Do you make black and white mistakes, not understanding everything about what it's like to be black? Because that's a big thing with Naomi Marie. I'm sure you know this, but she gets so mad at me for not knowing, for saying the wrong things. I'm trying to do better, but I just wondered how you're able to be . . . not making mistakes all the time."

Dad leans forward. "First of all, you may not know this, but I am older than you."

"That," I say, "is one of the few things I know for sure these days."

He tilts his head like a confused dog, but a sweet dog with a lot of sympathy in his eyes. "I know you're dealing with lots of change," he says, which *is* part of the problem, but only part. "Like I said, the things that are important to Valerie, to her girls, are very important to me. And I think it's important that our family do what we can to right the wrongs we see. But that's not a change. I've always talked about that."

Has he? I guess. Maybe I haven't been listening the right way. Or maybe I was too young. I still feel too young. And having a sister who's the same age but already knows so much makes me feel . . . less than. Less than her.

"And I just need to say one thing. I know I don't get my work done as fast, or get as good grades as her."

"Do you also know parents don't compare their children?"

"I know they're not supposed to, but I think they still do. And on top of that, feeling like I'm not nearly as smart as her, there's also the race stuff. I never thought about what color someone was before. I mean, obviously I noticed, but I didn't think about how their life, their every day, was different. I thought that meant I wasn't prejudiced or racist or whatever, but Naomi Marie has been very . . . um, helpful about pointing out the ways she thinks I am. All the things she sees that I don't. So did you always see it? Did Valerie have to show you? I don't really know yet how to be a good sister to Naomi Marie. And Brianna. And I want to be."

"A lot of this is because I didn't give you enough guidance. That's on me," he says. "I think maybe we expected those workshops to do more than a workshop can do, and I should have known better. Because I should have been tell-ing you that a good starting point for getting to know people, to understand a situation, is to listen to their stories, hear their fears, understand their lives, and to come together to improve the world as much as we can."

"Oh good," I say. "Simple." I'm joking, but I'm still think-ing it's all way too big, too much.

Dad tilts up my head so I'm looking at him. "That's the thing," he says. "Listening *is* simple. And listening is a way to bear witness, to be there when others are sharing their experiences. It's not a black or white thing. It's a good and important human thing that you're already doing. We're just going to work together to do it better."

I might have been hoping for a magic answer. But of course, there is none. I already knew I had a lot more to fig-ure out. At least now I know Dad will help me.

And if I want to do anything fun this weekend, I had bet-ter get some work done. So I leave Dad on the couch and go back to my room to look at that prompt again.

Can you point to a time in your life when you thought a certain way and then something or someone changed your thinking?

Naomi Marie.

It's not about peach ice cream or not liking school or liking Ketchup the cat. It's about Naomi Marie. Before I met her,

I thought that kids . . . were kids. That we went to school, hung out with friends, and if there was one thing that was important to us—like Annie with soccer—we did that too.

But Naomi Marie worries about social justice and . . . other things that always seemed more the kind of things grown-ups talked about. Like the way she's asking questions about that Cranstock guy. And how she knew that Jen saying "spirit animal" was wrong. I had no idea. The differences in the colors of our skin mean she has to worry about things I never knew to worry about.

I start writing about how it felt to be a kid before I met Naomi Marie, and when I get to the part about how Naomi Marie changed my thinking, I get a little stuck. Because the truth is, I know it should completely change my thinking, but it's truer to say that it's *starting* to change my thinking. Or maybe that I should change my thinking but I haven't been great at it yet. It all feels so big and hard and . . . way too grown-up for me. But I focus on what I find so amazing about her—the way she is this natural leader, this same-age-as-me person who knows so much—and I feel this little surge of pride in her.

I want cookies, but I make myself stay in my room and get it done, and I do the best I can. And for some reason, it isn't that hard. No color-coding needed.

CHAPTER THIRTY-NINE

Naomi Marie

It's been one of those weeks. The teachers are starting to give us so much homework that I actually don't finish most of it until I get home. I still haven't finished my "how my thinking has changed" essay; I hope no one finds out that I secretly asked Katherine for an extension. That's never happened before. I said hi to DeVante Swing and he said "Hi, Gigi." Oh, well. At least I gave Waverly the list I'd made about all the ways that she's special. She really liked "artist," and "thoughtful," and "upstander"—after I explained what that word meant. I told her to think of it as a "living document" that she could add to anytime.

Naomi E. and I are walking home from the train station, and a squirrel jumps in front of us to grab an acorn. Suddenly, it freezes and darts away through a gate into the day care center courtyard. Held on to that acorn, though.

"Hey, isn't that Lil Grizzy?" I ask, pointing to the tuxedo cat strolling down our block like he just bought a brownstone. "Why is he so far away from Ralph's?" Bodega cats usually stay close to their bodegas, where the food and the old-guy gossip is.

"No, I think that cat's a little bigger," says Naomi E. "And maybe his white patch is smaller?"

"*Duhhhh*, maybe it's actually a *girl* cat, *duhhhh*," says Bri. "You guys need to go back to kid-nergarden. *Duhhhh*."

I liked it better when she said "Question."

Momma meets us right at the door when we get home. "Welcome home, girls! Tom's making us a special dinner!"

Uh-oh.

"And by '*making*' you mean . . . ?" I ask.

"I mean I'm not quite sure what it is, but he's worked very hard, so let's be supportive, okay?"

"That's silly! Tom doesn't know how to cook, Momma," says Bri. "Everybody knows that—even Shelly Ann!"

"Shelly Ann knows what?" says Tom, walking out from the kitchen. He looks really sweaty. There's some kind of purplish sauce on his shirt. As *Idris Thompson, Teen Detective* would say: "This does not bode well."

"Guys, I'm sorry, I was trying to make us something special, but . . . it didn't quite work out."

"Yay!" yells Brianna, then "Ow!" after I elbow her.

Momma clears her throat. "Honey, thanks for trying, but . . ."

"But what?" says Tom.

"But THANK GOODNESS!" Momma says, and she starts laughing. After a beat, we all join in.

"Shake Shack?" asks Tom.

For once, Momma doesn't make us choose between fries and a shake, and we order both, but she says we have to have broccoli salad when we get home. Which is fine, because I love broccoli salad with apple bits and golden raisins and everything, and also because I made it yesterday and it's even sweeter and tangier the next day.

"Can we get Shelly Ann's on the way home too?" says Bri.

Momma just looks at her, and we move on.

"Nice try," I whisper to Bri. "I'm proud of you for recognizing opportunity. I'll show you how to make it work next time."

"Or Morningstar," she says to all of us. "I like that place too."

"I agree," I say, and Momma and Tom smile big. Our buzzer thing goes off, and they both go to get the food.

"Thanks for the Morningstar shout-out, Bri," says Naomi E.

"Maybe if we're *all* good, we can get Shelly Ann's AND Morningstar," says Bri, smiling even bigger than Momma and Tom.

I'm even more proud!

After we eat, we decide to walk home even though it's a little chilly. Momma and Bri go slow because Bri's trying to play a version of the license plate game that no one understands but only Momma has the patience for. Naomi E. walks with them, but she's wearing her hood up, which I know means she's listening to music while Bri says things like "Alaska! Peter's Chair! 5467819!"

Tom walks next to me. "How are things going at school?"

I shrug. "Okay," I say.

"Just okay?"

"Yes, just okay." I smile to let him know that I'm not trying to be difficult, and to remind him that talking to stepdads *is* difficult.

"And how do you feel about that?"

I sigh. Parents. I know he's using one of those *get-your-tween-to-open-up* techniques from a workshop. He and Momma don't realize that they always start talking like TV parents whenever they talk workshop talk. I know he's being nice. He *is* nice. And he's trying. I guess there's something in that.

"Well, the high schoolers were protesting because this guy

Josh Cranstock is giving money to the school—"

"Oh yes, the Eco-Casita thing . . ."

"Yeah, but apparently he also said some stuff once about how 'inner-city' kids should be in separate schools because they're not as smart as other kids."

Tom coughs. "That's pretty not-okay."

I nod. "Yeah. Not exactly those words, but I read some articles about it. Momma said he was 'dog whistling.'"

"You know, Naomi E. and I were talking," he says, "about differences, and how we're all learning to respect them, and how hard it is when people say or do things that are . . . disrespectful. Like that Jennifer girl. Or Cranstock."

"You mean racist?" I say, surprised.

"Yes," he says. "I mean racist. I don't know why I didn't just say that."

"You might not be used to saying it," I say, shrugging. "Anyway, hearing that he said that really bugs me, even though I think it would be good for us to have money for the Eco-Casita. I just wish it wasn't his money."

"I can understand why that might be a concern for you," says Tom.

"For me?"

"For *all* of us, for your school, our community," he responds. "You know, your mom taught me the phrase 'check your privilege' in one of her . . . personal workshops when we were dating."

I laugh. "I know about Momma's personal workshops. Last week, I got one about not looking up how to qualify for the National Spelling Bee until after I finished my regular homework."

"So, you know what I mean," says Tom, smiling. "The thing is, I was surprised, and I shouldn't have been. I hadn't thought much about my privilege for most of my life. It was just . . . my life. But the truth is, it's important that I do think about it. That I acknowledge that racism is a real part of American society. Not just a long time ago, but now."

We just keep walking. I turn back and see Bri trying to guide Momma toward a guy selling fruit snacks. Gold star for Bri today!

"Do you talk to Naomi E. about this stuff? Racism and privilege?" I ask after a while.

"Yes," says Tom.

"Sometimes it's hard when you do want to talk about it, but nobody wants to listen," I say.

"That's one thing I've learned about the first step to checking my privilege," Tom says. "It starts with listening. So . . . how's school going?" he asks again, and we both laugh a little.

"I'm not sure," I say. "I don't like being not sure, but middle school is more complicated than I thought it would be."

"Life goes that way, doesn't it," he says. "But more complicated doesn't necessarily mean bad."

"We don't need to go to any more workshops, Tom," I

say, smiling. "I think we can probably run our own."

He high-fives me. "Did I ever tell you I volunteered for Greenpeace when I was in college?"

"Yes," I say quickly. We stop and let the others catch up. We walk together for the rest of the way, and Naomi E. and I play Bri's game of jumping into little piles of leaves.

"Guys, guys, I was just telling Momma that we should get black-and-white cookies every day so we can remember that we're a Black-and-white family!" says Bri.

"And I was saying that I don't think we're going to forget," says Momma, and we all laugh.

Naomi E. looks like she's about to choke. "Is it okay to laugh about that?" she asks.

"About race?" says Momma. "Sure, when it's appropriate! The important thing is to talk about it. It's part of who we are, all of us. There are a lot of parts to each of us, and they all have value."

I think about how different Naomi E. is from Jennifer. At least Naomi E. wants to learn, wants a second chance. I still think it's not my job to teach her everything, but I can be supportive if she decides to teach herself. I think about books and music and computers and sewing and dancing and cake and broccoli—and how loving all those things at the same time is a part of who I am.

Yes, AND again, I guess. Yes, AND.

CHAPTER FORTY

Naomi E.

I hate to admit it, but some nights—not all, though—Dad's color-coding-workshop idea actually helps. If I do one quick assignment and one long one and take a short break, even though I'm taking a break, it takes less time. Because I don't have to focus on everything at once, which makes me . . . unfocused.

Long-term assignments and the endless revisions Katherine has me doing have a way of hanging over you, taking the good time you should be having and covering it with a thick coat of guilt about the work you're *not* doing. And even though I still have some math to finish up, I'm feeling pretty good.

Luckily, Edie also left her math homework for lunch, so we're in the same boat. She's scribbling down her work, and I'm staring out the window. Some of the trees are already all-the-way bare. There are piles of brown leaves everywhere.

"I still have seven problems left," she says.

"Yeah, I have a bunch too," I say. "But we'll get it done. We always . . . we almost always do." I'm getting better at working even when there are distractions around. And it's so nice to be with a friend, doing the same thing together, not crazy-worried about always being behind.

"Shoot," she says. "I actually have eleven problems left."

Math is not Edie's greatest strength.

One lucky thing: I'm not dreading getting my assignment back from Katherine, because I'm used to it now. She lists the many ways my work falls short, I listen, and I try again. It's routine now—nothing to fear.

Until I walk into the classroom. Because now it's all I can think about. And then I get a really sick feeling. And sure enough, it goes the same way it always does. She passes out our corrected assignments. She hands back a paper to Jen, who looks at her grade and grins, then shows it to Naomi Marie, who shuts her down with a stare that says, *I DO NOT CARE ABOUT YOUR GRADE.* I actually start to laugh, and Naomi Marie smiles quickly at me as I pretend to turn that laughter into a cough.

But Naomi Marie does care about her grades. It's not a

secret. And I watch a smile creep across her face when she gets her paper back. She puts it on her desk and goes through the pages, reading each comment, nodding, writing some notes of her own down.

And I don't get mine back.

Of course.

It's an easy period, at least. The people who want to can read their memoirs aloud. It's kind of interesting the different moments and people other kids wrote about—Gruber's next-door neighbor made him realize that not all Jets fans are horrible people. He honestly didn't know that until he was in fifth grade? Okay, Gruber.

I keep waiting for Naomi Marie to read, because I know how everyone would look at her, nodding and snapping, and how she'd have every person's attention. But we run out of time before she gets a turn.

I try to push down the awful feeling of knowing I tanked another assignment. Because once you do poorly, you have to keep writing new drafts, trying to do better, extra work. It's endless.

When the bell rings, Katherine calls me over to her desk. I'm still gathering my things when Jen bumps into me, totally on purpose, and loud-whispers, "Who'd have thought *you'd* be the Naomi who can't even do her work right?"

Words just fall out of my mouth. "Wow, Jen. What an incredibly racist thing to say. Who'd have thought you could be so many kinds of awful?"

Jen's mouth is open and she's trying to block my way, but Katherine calls over, "Is there a problem?" I'd like to tell her a problem or two, but I walk over to her desk, and at some point Jen leaves.

"This won't take long," Katherine says.

It never does.

She reaches out to touch my arm, and I think, *How weird—teachers never touch.* But maybe she does it to make me look at her face. When I do, she says, "This was extraordinary, Naomi E. When I read this the first time, all I could think was that I couldn't wait for you to share it with the class. But when I read it again, I realized maybe this is a more private kind of memoir, perhaps too delicate with both writer and subject in the same class. And I'll be discussing this in class next time, but I was thinking that students should be allowed to give some indication if they don't want to share, a private designation of some kind."

I nod, because she should have always had that. "That would be great," I say.

"But just look, Naomi E. Look what you are capable of! Haven't I been telling you this was inside you?"

I start to read the first page.

The first time I met my sister, we didn't know we'd be sisters. Everyone was focused on how funny it was that we had the same name.

My life changed when we met. Or maybe that's when it started to change.

We have the same name. We are the same age. And even though we live in the same yellow house, she lives in a different world than me. A bigger one. And often a harder one, I think. She sees things I don't see. And she has made me want to be able to see them too.

I'm still figuring it all out. I have a lot of work to bring my "racial lens" into focus. (We went to lots of workshops, so I know lots of terms, I just haven't figured out how to use them in my regular life.)

The thing about Naomi Marie is she is almost bigger than life. And when I'm not wasting time feeling a little lost in her enormous shadow, she makes me want to live a bigger life too.

So she changed me, not just the way I think about something—the way I think about everything. I am trying to . . . grow. I have a long way to go, but I have my eyes on the best, truest teacher there could be. And I'm ready to listen, and to learn.

"Forgive me for being nosy, but what did Naomi Marie say when she read it?"

"When she read it?" I ask, practically choking. "No, she hasn't—read it! You know that private-designation thing you said we could have? I think I need that with my sister a little too."

288

"I think you should show it to her."

It makes me think of when Naomi Marie let me see that she had a list of things she liked about me when I was stuck on my origin story assignment, and how I wondered if she had to make that list because she needed reminding. Even if that was the case, I felt good knowing the list was so long.

And it actually feels pretty good to think about showing this memoir assignment to her too. Someday.

CHAPTER FORTY – ONE

Naomi Marie

Xio's coming over after school and so is Gigi, and I'm so happy but also scared about my worlds colliding. We're all going to do the first episode of the Global Girls vlog. I figure if we make it first and it's amazing, which it will be, then I can convince Momma to let me have a vlog.

I finally figured out what to write for my "how my thinking has changed" memoir. Last night I watched this fancy author do a talk about "the danger of the single story." I really liked the part where she said that it's not that the single story isn't true, "it's that it's incomplete." Like how Waverly is angry; and she's also a great artist and sensitive and funny too. I think that's how my thinking has changed—I don't have to pick one self; I can be all of my selves at once, or at different times. Sometimes people (often named Jennifer) won't get it, but I get to choose. I get to decide who I am and who to share myself with. I will not be *terraformed* just because someone else isn't comfortable with all of me. Poor Katherine. She said five hundred words. I know I'm going long. Momma has always taught me that it's better to write *more* than *less*. She also told me not to tell my teachers she said that, though.

At lunch I notice that Gigi is wearing an outfit I never saw before: red leggings with cats on them, a blue mini skirt, and a yellow hoodie that says *SUPERHERO* in glitter letters.

"Cute outfit!" I say.

"Do you think Xio will like it?"

"Absolutely," I say. "But she's not the type to judge people by their clothes, you know."

"I know; it's just that you're always talking about her and how she's your best friend and how cool she is. . . . I just want us to get along."

I hug her. "Xio is going to LOVE you and you are going to LOVE her and I LOVE you both—and of course, you both LUVVVVV me, so we're all good," I say.

"Gross," says a voice behind us. Gruber's on recycling duty, so he's holding a bucket filled with half-eaten food ready to compost. "Oh, Naomi Marie the Black Sister," says Gruber suddenly, "I read that Jumbies book you told me about. It was pretty good. Are there any more?"

I ignore the very literal nickname and say, "Yeah! The sequel's even better: *Rise of the Jumbies*! And if you like scary, try *Spirit Hunters*. It is awesomely creepy."

"Yeah, thanks," he mumbles. "Are you guys going up to the library?"

"Um . . . yeah," I say, even though Gigi is poking me in a definite NO NO NO way. "Um, maybe we'll see you up there."

Gruber just rolls his eyes and makes like he's about to dump the bucket on us. Lori, who's on lunchroom duty today, swoops in out of nowhere and hauls him off, to a round of snaps from everyone in the vicinity.

This group has gotten into the habit of heading up to the library every few days; it's not officially a club or anything, which is kind of what I wanted to do, so we could have rules and officers and plans, but Daisuke and Momma and everyone in the group said they thought we should just leave things relaxed and casual. Oh, well. I can still start clubs at Ms. Starr's library.

"Hey, are you guys leaving?" It's Naomi E. We haven't had lunch together in a while. When school started, I thought we'd have the same friends, the same life, the same everything.

It hasn't been like that. It's been better and surprising and lonelier all at once. Part of adjusting my vision without compromising my principles has definitely meant letting two itchy feelings exist at the same time.

Gigi grabs my stuff. "I'll take your trash and meet you in the library."

After she moves away, Naomi E. turns to me. "Gigi's cool. I like her."

"She and Xio are coming over after school," I say.

"Oh yeah, I remember," says Naomi E. "I have a Drama Club meeting, but I hope I get back in time to see Xio."

"Yeah." I pause. "We're doing a thing about kids and activism."

"Is it another club?" she asks. "Are you working on setting a club-starting record? I'm pretty sure you already have."

"Ha-ha. Nope, just . . . friends doing something. You can hang out with us when you get home."

"Maybe Edie and I will join you guys in the library?" says Naomi E., like she's not sure.

I shrug and smile. Two different things at the same time. "Sure, that would be nice. You're always welcome. *And* no pressure."

"You know I want to be there for you, right?" she says quickly. "I'm learning how."

"I know, and I appreciate that. And I appreciate you." I say. Sometimes workshop talk, well, *works*. "I want to be there for you too."

The lunchroom is starting to empty as people head to the yard for recess.

"I'm on board with anything that's important to you," says Naomi E.

"I want you to be on board with things not just because of me, but because they're important to *you*," I say. "And if we have different ideas about what's important, we'll work it out. We've got time."

"Let's just do it ourselves, though," she says. "If the parents find out, you know we'll be in a workshop in minutes."

I nod. "Sisterhood in a New Hood: Navigating the Rocky Waters of New Spaces and Places," I say, giggling.

"Finding the Third Way for Blended Families: When the Best Choice Is None at All," she says.

"And we'd have to keep dialogue journals," I say. "Which I actually love. Me and Momma do one."

"I know," she replies. "She asked me if I wanted to do one too."

I wonder if that's going to be weird, Momma doing a journal with Naomi E. I think it's just going to be *more*. Maybe good and bad, up and down, itchy and scratchy— Wait, that's the same. Maybe I won't mind as much as I would have before. Like Yes, AND. Like complicated, in a good, growing way. Like sisters.

"Here's a tip," I say. "Mention Morningstar at least once a week. I always do that for Shelly Ann's."

"Nice," she says. "And then we can coordinate and get both."

Different, but together. Working on it.

We hug, and then I head upstairs to my meeting. I don't know if Naomi E. will make it, but that's okay. I've got people there, and I'll see her at home. And we'll talk some more.

Momma picked up Bri after school to give me a little freedom to travel home with my real best friends and not Bri's invisible ones, who are okay most of the time, but still.

Me and Gigi head over to the Walgreens near my subway stop to wait for Xio. I'm excited, but a little scared that

> Xio will talk about all the things we used to do (back in the day) and make Gigi feel left out.
> Gigi will talk about all the new people in my life that Xio doesn't know, and make Xio feel left out.
> I won't know what to say or do, so Gigi and Xio will realize that the one thing they have in common is thinking I'm not cool, and *I'll* be left out.

I wish Naomi E. were here; she'd remind me to be all nonchalant and say that it'll all work out if I just go with the flow. Hearing her imaginary voice in my head saying exactly that helps.

What ends up happening is that Xio gets to Walgreens at

almost the same exact time as we do and we all hug and laugh and scream a little, and Mrs. Lowe waves from her steps, and then the three of us walk home together like we've been doing it all our lives.

Momma makes Xio and Gigi call their parents ("No texting") as soon as we get in the doorway. Xio gives her "a gift from my mom," a bag of frozen pasteles en hoja—yes! Momma really came through with the snacks. Mini beef patties, hummus from Sahadi's, and cheese samboosak from Damascus bakery. She's got cut-up veggies in a muffin tin, and there's even a tea tray with a pot of ginger tea and homemade apple cake.

"Save some for your sister," says Momma. "Girls," she says to Xio and Gigi, "I'm putting some beef patties aside for you to bring home."

"Where is Naomi E., by the way?" asks Xio. "I took pics of my room to show her. I want to give it a makeover."

"She's at Drama Club, but she'll be here soon," I say. "And you'll get to meet her friend Edie; she's coming over too. She's cool; she knows the value of a good cheese-and-tomato sandwich."

"Mmmm," says Xio, right as Gigi says, "Yuck." Guess they're not totally in sync.

Momma says *just this once* we can bring some snacks into the bedroom if we spread a picnic blanket. Woot! She heads to Bri's room to play Buffaloes in Space School. We hid that book about teaching a buffalo to play drums, but Bri memorized it anyway.

"I have an important question," I say. "Do you want to form a team for the citywide Geography Bowl competition?"

Gigi and Xio look at each other.

"Will *you* think about *Vocalympian* Round One auditions?" asks Xio.

"Oooh, I LOVE *Vocalympians!*" says Gigi.

"Do you mean coming with you for moral support, or actually, like, singing?" I say.

"Singing!" they both say.

"I've already picked out a name: Threedom," says Xio.

"Did you just make that up right now?" I ask.

"Three of us, freedom . . . ," she replies. Gigi nods like it all makes sense.

"Well, we should ask Naomi E. and Edie if they want to do it," I say. It sounds like maybe the last thing Naomi E. would want to do. Like maybe even after writing a book report. And Friday Laundry Night. But still. I'm always going to ask.

"Okay then, Fifth . . . Dimension!"

"The Tesseract!" says Gigi, and we explain to Xio why that works in a "Wrinkle in Time" way.

We start brainstorming about Global Girls topics that will be interesting to girls our age around the world.

"Can we take a break to talk integers?" says Gigi after a while. "Because I need help with the math homework."

"And why do they call them rational numbers?" Xio says. "The whole thing is seriously irrational!"

"I know it's Friday, but . . ." I'm a little embarrassed, but I remember what Naomi E. said on the first day at school about giving myself a chance to just be. "I mean . . . we *could* do some homework. Just for a little while, until Naomi E. and Edie get here." I hold my breath.

"Perfect!" says Gigi. And she's not joking!

"I figured you'd say that, and my mom said I had to do at least one assignment, so I'm ready," says Xio. "And it's more fun to do it together anyway."

Which is what we do. It feels like two minutes go by, and suddenly Naomi E. and Edie are in the doorway.

"Are you guys doing *homework*?" asks Naomi E.

I nod. "Would you like to join us? How was Drama Club?"

"As you can see, the party never ends around here," Naomi E. says to Edie, who smiles and waves. Naomi E. turns back to me. "And I think we *will* join you. I mean, more homework now means less on Saturday morning."

"You never do homework on Saturday morning," I say.

"Okay, okay, Sunday," she says. "I was just trying to sound supportive."

"Thanks," I say, laughing. "And I do want to know about

Drama Club. I still think you should audition for a part."

"And I still think doughnuts should be three of the four food groups, but no one agrees with that either."

"I do," says Edie.

"Me too," says Gigi.

"Can't say you're wrong," Xio chimes in.

"Doughnuts *and* cake," I say. "Bam!"

"Are you guys ganging up on me?" says Naomi E.

"Of course not," I say. "We're being supportive." I wiggle my eyebrows.

Before we get back to integers and rational numbers, I think about this show that Momma lets me stream for Friday-night TV choice time. In the theme song, there's a line like "I'm glad I've got my girls." And that's how I feel.

Really, really glad.

CHAPTER FORTY - TWO

Naomi E.

The yellow house is overfull, but in the very best way. It's filled with friends—with Edie, and Xio and Gigi. Next time everyone gets together like this, we'll have to do it when Annie can come too. Seeing Xio and Gigi together makes me realize that Yes, AND works, even beyond the rules of a new family coming together.

I can't help wondering what year-ago me would have thought of all this. It would have seemed absolutely impossible. I loved my life then—the quiet, the way it was so predictable. But there's something really nice about this sweet yellow house filled with life—messy, random, not-always-easily-resolved life.

I'm trying to spread out this giant piece of fabric on the blank wall in our room. It needs to look really good but not so good that it's distracting for the Global Girls vlog. Xio and Gigi are still working on the theme song, but today we're putting together a video asking girls from different parts of the world to send us videos explaining what their lives are like.

I wonder how many we'll get. And how specific they'll be. I wonder if two same-named people from different races are learning to be a family on the other side of this earth. Or in New Jersey. Or are we the only two people to ever go through something exactly like this?

"Please, please, please can I come out now?" Brianna calls from the other side of her door, even though Valerie is in there with her, probably telling her she can't. "I never get to see Xio, and I want to get to know Gigi and Edie and—"

I open the door. Brianna stumbles a little—I guess she was right up against it. "I need your help," I say. "Need" might not be the actual truth, but I know it's nice to feel needed, like an important part of a family.

Valerie smiles at me. "Come back when you're done, Brianna," she says.

"I won't be done for a long time, Momma. You don't need to wait."

While everyone else is rooting about in the kitchen,

scraping out every last crumb of that delicious apple cake, I show Brianna how I need her to tack the fabric to the wall behind the dresser, where none of us can reach.

"Save me some apple cake," I yell.

"Probably not happening," Edie yells back.

"Too good to share," Gigi says.

Brianna sighs. "I'll do this," she says, her hand and part of her head behind the dresser, "but then I want to do better things."

Yeah, me too. Like get my hands on that cake.

She's reaching out her hand for the second tack when Naomi Marie, Xio, Gigi, and Edie come back into the room. "Got it," Brianna says, and crawls back out.

"Oh look," Edie says. "It's the third Naomi."

Brianna smiles but then sort of shakes her head like she's changing her mind. "Actually," she says, "I don't really want to be a Naomi anymore."

Xio laughs. "No. You just want to be with them all the time and hang out with their friends all the time and EAT OUR SNACKS!" She's laughing. But Brianna isn't.

"I mean it," Brianna says. "Naomis have fights; one was so big that White Naomi went home sick from school even though maybe I'm not sure she was sick. And Naomi Marie didn't eat any of her lunch that day, EVEN THE CAKE—she brought it all home! And she thought nobody could tell she was crying in the bathroom and not peeing, but I know the difference. But you know what I'm talking about," she says, looking at Naomi Marie, "when you used your grown-up Serious voice," and then looking at me, "and you were both crying?"

The room was already pretty quiet, but it goes a whole other kind of quiet. And then, at the same instant, everyone tries to fill the silence. Edie apologizes for finishing the apple cake and Xio is asking Naomi Marie if everything is okay. And I'm sure that's what everyone is wondering after Brianna's report from the dark side.

"Everything *is* okay," I say. "We had some stuff, some really hard stuff to work out. And we're still working on it," I say.

"And we always will," Naomi Marie says. "I mean, we always will talk it out. Or work it out. Or wait it out, until we do . . . that other talking-and-working stuff."

"But for now," Xio says, "we should get started, because that . . . tapestry or whatever it is you put on the wall is a perfect backdrop for our intro."

"And we're almost done with the theme song," Gigi says.

"I want to hear it!" Brianna says. And then she looks at Edie and says, "Did you say you ate all the apple cake?"

Edie looks so guilty, like she ate up every little kid's Halloween candy and left them only the little root-beer-flavored lollipops.

"Momma! Where are you hiding? You have to take me to

Shelly Ann's. I didn't get any cake, and it's not fair!"

"Well done, Edie," Naomi Marie says.

"Let's do this while we still can," I say.

And I feel this wave surge inside me, the excited feeling of being part of something new. Not just this family, but this group of friends that wants to create something together and to hear other people's stories, to share them. And to appreciate the wonder of apple cake and other delicious baked goods. Together.

EPILOGUE

NM: Hiiiiii.

NE: . . . I thought I was supposed to be doing this dialogue thing with your mom. Are we going to do this every night?

NM: Isn't this exciting? It's like old-school texting!

NE: Why don't we just text?

NM: This is more fun. But we have to come up with a system.

NE: A system of what? Also we're sitting right next to each other doing this. Doesn't that defeat the purpose?

NM: Okay, okay . . . I'll take it over to my bed first. . . . So, we should have special notebooks, and pens. . . .

NE: Special pens?

NM: Oooh! And a special code word.

NE: Don't even use the word CODE. The parents might hear.

NM: Sorry to break it to you, but we're totally doing the GGTS Winter Break workshop.

NE: Noooooooooooooooooooooooooooooooooooooooo!

NM: It's going to be great. We should start making a list of game ideas. Xio's doing it too. Maybe I'll ask Gigi. I bet Edie would be in.

NE: I hate to say it, but you could be right. . . . She just might be.

NM: Of course I'm right!

NE: Uh-huh.

NM: Are you just agreeing because you're sleepy? EEEEEEEEEEEEEEEE!

NE: Sorry. And I hate to admit it, but E doesn't bother me as much as it used to.

NM: Oh. Then I'll come up with something else.

NE: You really are a big sister.

NM: And now, so are you!

NE: Listen, I just want you to know that I'd never try to take your place or anything.

NM: It's not EITHER/OR. . . .

NE: I know, I know. Yes, AND. We should get T-shirts.

NM: YESSS!

NE: I was kidding.

NM: We'll revisit. So . . . have you decided what to call Momma? She just wants you to be comfortable.

NE: My mouth can't call her Valerie yet. But maybe someday.

NM: True. Maybe come up with something totally new. We're making exceptions, building new traditions, remember?

NE: Yeah . . . I'm just nervous. Every step in our new life feels like a giant step, and I don't want to . . . misstep, you know?

NM: That was kind of poetic, E! You're going to get an Honors in Creative Writing.

NE: All I did was use the word STEP a lot.

NM: Let me compliment you, please. Anyway, I feel the same way. New family, new house, new school . . . it's like you think you're going to fall off into nothingness. Into a great void— Hey! No trying to grab the dialogue journal!

NE: I got the point, okay?

NM: Okay, okay. Brown thumbs-up emoji

NE: You can't write "brown thumbs-up emoji." And again, we could just text instead of throwing this notebook back and forth.

NM: Side-eye emoji

NE: Stop.

NM: Let's decide now that any time we're mad at each other, we go to Shelly Ann's AND Morningstar to work it out over cake.

NE: Deal. And when we're happy with each other too.

NM: Deal. So, you're loving this, aren't you?

NE: If I say yes, can we go to sleep?

NM: Just say yes first.

NE: Yes.

NM: Yes, AND . . . laughing emoji. Okay, good night.

NE: Sigh. But okay: laughing emoji. Good night.

Acknowledgments

We owe a great debt of gratitude to Kristin Daly Rens, who always saw through to the heart of the story. Kristin, your ever-patient, thoughtful, and loving care of the Naomis was a constant boost, and we are so grateful that no one has to know what a mess this book was until you unraveled, appraised, and guided us to fix it. You even made the conversations about all the work we had to do engaging. We will be forever thankful.

Kelsey Murphy: many thanks for the abundance of assists and all your good cheer along the way.

Renée Cafiero and Andrea Curley, sorry we made you work so hard, but thank you very much for your invaluable assistance.

To Erin Murphy, thank you for remembering the Naomis on that fateful day and knowing Kristin was the right person for the job.

To our Balzer + Bray family, thank you so much for

supporting the Naomis, spreading the word, and being so wonderful to work with.

To the We Need Diverse Books team, thank you so much for shining a light on our stories, and for centering all the beautiful stories that are often pushed to the margins.

To the Nerd Camp crews in New Jersey and Long Island, the #BookJourney team, Donalyn Miller, John Schumacher, Preeti Chhibber, Ann Marie Wong, Dhonielle Clayton, Ellen Oh, and all the teachers, librarians, parents, and friends who have brought the Naomis into libraries, classrooms, and homes: We have so much appreciation for you and the work you do every day. Thank you for having hard conversations with hope, for celebrating the power of story, and for empowering young readers.

And finally, to the readers of all ages who embraced the Naomis, who believe in the power of books—each and every one of you shines so beautifully and powerfully. Thank you for reading and sharing your thoughts, and especially for inspiring us every day.

Keep Reading!

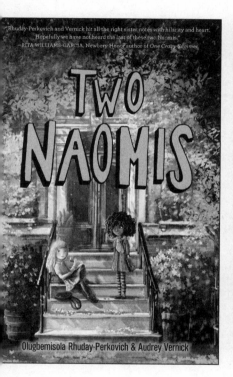